# SOME LIKE IT SCANDALOUS

## GOING ROYAL
### BOOK TWO

HEATHER LONG

*For Virg.*
*My first, and best, Going Royal fan.*
*I wrote this for her birthday after all.*

# FOREWORD

Dear Reader,

Thank you for picking up *Some Like it Scandalous*. If this is your first book you've picked up from me, welcome, happy to have you along for the ride! If you've read me for a while, you might be thinking this is a very familiar title, and you wouldn't be wrong. The first draft of this book dates back to 2012. It was later contracted by Carina Press, a digital imprint of Harlequin as the second in the Going Royal series and released in 2014.

This book does what I loved about so many similar series I read while growing up, takes a connected character from the first book and tells their story, their romance. It's also a second chance romance which is one of my all-time favorite tropes.

Anna and Armand, like Alyx and Daniel before them, are a bit of a rom com couple. Their chemistry was just right there from the first crackling scene. A scene late in the book featuring a Nerf gun is my favorite for this particular installment. Yes, each book in the Going Royal series contains a favorite scene.

Re-reading this as I went through to edit, punch up some scenes, update the tech, and references, I kept forgetting what I was doing and just *read* the book. It's a treat when I get to enjoy something I wrote and I have enough distance from when I wrote it to *really* enjoy it.

Still, I am so excited to share this with you and I hope you enjoy this little throwback to a different style of storytelling.

Happy reading!

xoxo

Heather

# CHAPTER I
## ANNA

The five-thousand-dollar painting on the wall hung crookedly. Not so much as to be obvious but—since she'd stared at it for the last fifteen minutes cooling her heels—she'd noticed. Anna Novak slanted a look down at the scratched face of her wristwatch.

*Twenty minutes.*

Her blood pressure rose. She hated waiting. She liked it even less when it followed a summons that came via special messenger with specific orders to arrive by two in the afternoon or consider their offer to fund the scholarship ended.

The only reason to stipulate punctuality and make her wait was power.

The grand duke had flexed his royal muscles to teach her a lesson. The crooked angle of the picture added to the steady thrum of a headache pounding against the backs of her eyes. She walked away from the expensive leather sofa and the plush rug to stare out the window. The Petersburg Tower parked squarely in the center of Los Angeles boasted an amazing view from its thirtieth floor. She could make out the Pacific Ocean in the distance, beyond the filmy haze hovering over the area.

She stared at the water, imagining herself standing on the sandy beach. The wind would push her hair back from her face and the water would lap at her bare feet. It didn't matter that it was cold. The gentle ebb and flow of the tide reminded her even the worst storms passed.

"Ms. Novak?" A pleasant feminine voice pulled her attention back to the luxurious surroundings. Turning, she saw Gretchen, the blonde secretary who'd greeted her at the elevator and escorted her into the waiting room. "His Highness is ready to see you now. Please follow me."

Shifting the strap of her purse against her shoulder, Anna claimed her laptop bag and followed—not that Gretchen left her with much choice. *It's not her fault he kept you waiting.* No, it absolutely wasn't. That didn't help assuage her temper much. *You'll catch more flies with honey than vinegar.*

She would catch even more with horse manure, but she fought to maintain her composure. The scholarship fund needed the additional checks the royal family pledged to Princess Alyxandretta's start-up project. Key phrase in the sentence was *needed*, not wanted. If Anna had realized when she took the job who she would be working for...

Cutting off that thought, she pasted on a plastic smile. The hallway continued the tribute to the grand duke's magnificent wealth. Masterful artwork—mostly Russian impressionists—decorated the walls with expensive designer vases stationed every third painting. The carpet muffled the sound of her heels. It didn't take her long to realize Gretchen led her to the pair of cherry-colored oaken doors at the end of the hall. The paneled wood cried out *ornate elegance.*

Breathing became optional the closer she came and her heart thundered like a horse galloping full tilt to escape. Dread cramped her stomach.

This couldn't be any worse than walking to her execution.

*Of course, I could have had a last meal instead of a stale granola bar and the cold coffee leftover from the drive into the office this morning.*

Gretchen grasped both handles and pushed the doors wide. She curtsied with exquisite grace. "Anna Novak, Your Highness."

Anna's heart leaped. She searched the expensive—and spacious—office, desperate to see him before he saw her. But she didn't have to search long. He stood with his back to the door, gazing out of a massive picture window. If the view from the waiting room was magnificent, this one took her breath away. The Los Angeles valley seemed to sprawl out at his feet, as though waiting for him to step down from the glass tower and walk among the mortals.

"Thank you, Gretchen. That will be all." He

didn't turn and Gretchen curtsied once more. And then she was gone, the doors closing silently, but the latch of the two coming together echoed through Anna. The figure he cut against the glass was impressive, tall and lean. His shoulders seemed even broader somehow and his dark— silky as sin—hair stopped just above his collar. He stood with his hands clasped behind his back.

Anna considered her options. She could speak, but that probably flew in the face of protocol. Not that she was altogether certain she could push words out past the lump in her throat. It had been a bad idea to come.

*An extremely bad idea.*

Maybe if she were quiet enough, she could open one of the doors and slip out the way she came. Her expertise in managing charities and organizations included fundraising. She could continue trying to get money elsewhere.

"Miss Novak." He turned and not even the backlight of the broad windows could overshadow the patrician nose, the square jaw, the high forehead and the spectacularly devastating black eyes. His gaze struck her like a physical blow, pinning her in place. Her heart punched her ribs and spots danced in front of her eyes. Her chest squeezed and memories she spent years trying to bury swarmed through her mind.

*"I like it, what do you think?" He stood a foot back from the brown sofa they rescued from a dumpster earlier in the day and stared at the picture of four pandas playing poker he hung above it.*

*"It's not centered." Arguably it was completely off center, angled over the far right seat.*

*"It is centered—to the room." He tossed a grin over his shoulder. The European accent still peeked through his words. It faded some in the two years they dated, but whenever something annoyed him...*

*"The room doesn't have enough in it to justify centering it to the room. It should go over the middle of the sofa." She padded barefoot across the floor. "Or, easier still, we move the sofa." She put her weight against the edge and shoved it down the wall until the pandas centered over the middle cushion. Spinning to show off her work, she slammed up against his chest. His mouth slanted over hers and swallowed her squeal.*

*They went down in a tangle of arms and legs. It didn't take long to forget all about the picture.*

She shook her head, rousing from melancholy-laced desire. She *could* do this. She *would* do it. The scholarship fund needed the money. Her pride didn't help anyone and it wasn't like he could shatter her heart twice. "Good afternoon, Your Highness."

He stared at her. Did he see the same images of the past or had his long parade of mistresses effectively stamped out all remaining footprints of the life—*no, not life, lie*—the lie they lived?

"Please. Have a seat." He coughed once and stepped forward, stretching out an arm to indicate the conversation pit created by a rectangular collection of sofas and love seats. She pivoted, grateful to not have to keep staring at him.

Ten years eroded the last traces of his boyish youth, but the man left in his place...

Dizzy possibility assaulted her. Did he still take his coffee with heavy doses of cream? Did he still prefer chicken sandwiches to burgers? Had he given up the penchant for eating every single french fry or waking up the middle of the night in search of something salty and sweet? Popcorn and caramel chocolates were—had been—his favorites, mixed together until their hands were sticky with it, but they'd always managed to lick each other clean.

Pinching the bridge of her nose, she wished she could tear the images off and discard them. The dull headache plaguing her earlier roared to life and beat in time with her pulse.

"Are you alright?" He caught her elbow and she flinched, pulling away swiftly.

"Don't touch me." She glared at him, the pain sending spots back to decorate her vision.

The concern on his face hardened and the temperature of his voice dropped. "Have a seat. I will get you some water." His accent tipped each word, rolling the vowels.

*Good.* He annoyed her too.

She didn't want to sit, but she didn't want to embarrass herself any further by falling. She compromised by perching on the edge of the farthest cushion, angled so she could rise and, if necessary, flee. Charlie—the *prince*— She curled her fingers, digging her nails against her palms. He wasn't Charlie. He was the Grand Duke Armand Dagmar, a prince.

*And a lying bastard...*

Pain scored along her soul, but she lifted her chin. Cobbling together the scraps of her pride, she wielded it like a flimsy shield. The prince returned with a pair of water bottles and two heavy crystal glasses. He set them on the polished wood center table without any coasters. She cringed at the damage the water spots might do. A stack of heavy wood squares sat on the end table next to her. Peeling her fingers off the handle to her laptop bag, she set it down and reached for two wooden squares.

The prince said nothing as she placed a coaster under each one. He loosened a button holding his suit jacket together and sat with careless grace in the chair to her right. The warmth of his leg grazed hers and it took every ounce of will not to jerk again as though scalded. Reacting revealed her weakness—she couldn't afford it. So she endured the casual contact, taking her time to shift her leg away.

Charlie—*dammit*, the prince—opened her bottle and held it out to her. Steeling herself, she met his gaze. One corner of his mouth curved upward in the vaguest hint of a smile. "Do you still prefer it from the bottle?"

*He remembers...* "No. A glass will be fine," she lied, slamming shut the window to the past. It was enough to hang on to her sense of self and they'd barely spoken a dozen words to each other. His gaze shuttered, the warmth draining away. With a nod, he poured the water into the glass, filling it three-quarters before capping the water bottle and repeating the process with his own. Tumbler in hand, he took a long drink like it held vodka. Instead of saying anything, he stared at her moodily.

She clasped her hands together, not quite trusting the trembling in her fingers. The longer he stared at her, the more her resolve eroded. "Your Highness? You requested this meeting."

"I did." He nodded slowly and his expression darkened, a veil dropping over the man she thought she knew and leaving only the royal leader he became behind. "You are the director of the Princess Alyxandretta's scholarship fund for foster children."

It wasn't a question. He took another drink, draining the glass before setting it on the table— next to the coaster. His midnight gaze collided with hers and her imagination seemed to be playing tricks on her. She thought she saw the humor there—as though he teased her.

*It's his table, if he wants to ruin it...* She ignored the glass, refusing the bait. "I am."

"An interesting choice of occupation." Still not a question.

Resting her hands on her lap, she lifted her brows and waited.

Irritation creased his perfectly pleasant expression. "What are your qualifications for the position?"

"None of your business." She smiled politely. "I interviewed with the board and Mrs. Voldakov. They were all satisfied with my qualifications and hired me."

"Of course, however, the scholarship fund is in the process of being relocated under the Dagmar Foundation and you have not been interviewed by the head of the foundation." Every word perfectly enunciated and emphasized by his accent. The angrier he grew, the more formal his speech became—or at least that was how it had been. His temper lurked beneath that placid surface.

Her stomach plummeted. The relocation of the fund could only mean a new direction, new oversight and more paperwork. She'd just finished getting the nonprofit status fully vetted, and they remained in probation status on their grant applications. Changes meant those applications would become null and void.

"I see." *Play it cool. You can do this.* The internal cheerleader lacked any real confidence and cool sweat dampened her back. Thank God the jacket she wore hid the unpleasant reaction. Sliding her purse to rest on the sofa next to her thigh, she retrieved her laptop case. Fortunately, the designer bag offered numerous pockets and storage capacity for her files. Violently aware of the prince's gaze on her, she thumbed through the contents and pulled out three quarter-inch-thick manila folders. Returning the case to the floor, she flipped open the first file and extracted her résumé. She set it on the table between them.

"My qualifications and work history." She added a stack of six sheets. "Personal references." And finally, a three-page letter of introduction from the previous fund she'd administered. "Professional recommendation."

The prince ignored the stack. "I did not ask for your résumé or your letters of reference. I want to know why *you* think you're qualified to do this job."

"And you'll find my qualifications are outlined quite clearly in those papers." What did he want from her?

"I find that it's easy to disguise shortcomings with a cleverly phrased sentence. Harder to compensate in person." He couldn't have slapped her harder if he'd reached out to strike her.

*How dare he?* She stood, barely catching the folders before paper slid free from them. Incensed, she glared at him. "You're one to accuse me of deception."

"Sit down, Miss Novak."

"I'd prefer to stand." Her lungs burned with every deep inhale. Her temper unraveled further at his too-calm gaze. She hated it when he tried to "handle" her.

"Sit. Down." The quiet command just pissed her off more and she grabbed her laptop bag, shoving the folders inside—ignoring him completely. It was a mistake to think she could do this—a mistake to believe that a decade could mute the betrayal.

"My apologies, Your Highness." Heat flooded her face. Her jaw ached from clenching her teeth. "I do not think this going to work out." And it made her sick to think she wouldn't be a part of the solution so many young men and women needed to achieve their educational dreams. Better to let someone else handle the royal arrogance and demand.

"Miss Novak...please..." He sighed.

She made it three steps.

"Stay. Please."

*Keep walking.* But she didn't. The quiet words took all the fire out of her sails.

She looked back. He stood, his hands in the pockets, but the neutrality in his expression evaporated. The quiet request accompanied by the all too familiar hopeful smile twisted the dagger in her heart.

"Go to hell, Charlie." The venom in the words startled her. Tears filled her eyes and she blinked furiously to keep them at bay. "I came here to do business, not to be interrogated like some supplicant to your throne. You could have sent someone else, but you made me come here as if I would bend one damn knee to you."

A knock at the door interrupted any response he might have made. She started forward and a man in a black-on-black suit that screamed security glanced in. "Forgive the interruption, Your Highness. We wanted to make sure everything was all right." The guard didn't look at the prince, though, his steely expression rested on her.

"We are having a mild disagreement, Nelson. Thank you, that will be all." The dismissal satisfied the guard and after one last hard look at her, he closed the door again.

Security had to be standing right outside the door—how else could they have heard her?

Would they keep her from leaving?

"Anna. Five minutes. Please." His voice wrapped lovingly around her name, a sensuous caress, and she halted, closing her eyes. The third please doused the flames of irritation.

*Five minutes.*

"Fine." She turned and set her bag down on the floor again. Glancing at her watch, she fought to remain impassive. The hell she would cry in front of him, no matter how raw and battered her heart. "You have five minutes."

He stood next to the chair he'd sat in and didn't try to approach her. Honestly, he didn't have to. She couldn't look away. "I have read your résumé and your letters of recommendation. I know why others believe you to be so qualified. But the success of this enterprise is extremely important to my cousin. Thus, it is important to me. You know she was in the foster care system— she benefited from scholarship programs—and she desperately wants to help others like herself."

Deeper emotion clouded those words—pride and regret. The latter sank a hook into her heart. "She explained. She's an amazing woman."

For the first time since she'd walked into the room, the prince smiled—truly smiled—and the warmth in it kindled heat in her belly. "She is. My only regret is the family did not know about her before the last several months. She holds no grudge against us, though I do. She believes you are a fantastic asset—her exact word was 'perfect.'"

His giving voice to someone else's compliment shouldn't have filled her with such an irrational sense of joy, but the swell of it punctured the outrage that fueled her earlier flight. "Mrs. Voldakov and I spent several hours chatting about her hopes for the project. I agree with her sentiment. It's a worthy cause and it provides a much-needed boost for those who might have to forgo further education because of financial hardship. I am intimately acquainted with the struggles of low-income families and those struggles are only magnified for foster children who lack the basic support structure for success."

If not for her own scholarships, she would likely be working in the same diner as her mother or the mechanic shop with her father. One of six children, Anna knew her parents' resources had been stretched to the breaking point. She'd saved her family money and still managed to chase her dreams.

*Well, some of them...*

"You worked hard for your scholarships. You pushed away personal commitments to achieve the grades you needed..." The prince stepped toward her.

"Thank you." All the moisture in her mouth dried up. "I had support. This scholarship—the foundation it can become—can provide that support to so many others. I know what it means to need."

Thankfully, he redirected and stopped at the edge of his desk and put a hand on the wooden edge. "You weren't recruited for this position. You applied. Why leave the organization you worked for to come to this one?"

The question puzzled her. Directors of large corporations moved around frequently. "It's an excellent opportunity."

"It is hours of intensive labor, compliance restrictions, and paperwork. Your previous project, Hart's House, provided support for abuse victims, educational and relocation opportunities, and you opened over fifty different establishments in major cities across the United States in the last five years—doubling not only their available working capital, but also the number of help hot spots." The full weight of his gaze rested on her, as though he evaluated her every reaction and she fought against fidgeting.

"You managed a brilliant opportunity—so, why give that up to take on a relatively small scholarship with years of work in front of it?" He held her gaze captive. The masculine intensity of him dominated the room. He'd done his homework—because not all of the information he recited had been in her résumé.

She sucked her lower lip between her teeth. Why give up one lofty, worthwhile project for another? She'd struggled with the decision for a month after submitting her application. "Hart House doesn't need me to succeed anymore. We have a fantastic array of directors, city managers and political support. My assistant director handled most of the day-to-day operations and she can and will manage it beautifully. I'm not averse to hard work and this scholarship program—the whole basis of the foundation—needs people who believe in the system of success it can provide. Who know it can be more than just a dream or a fairytale."

"Of course." He sounded...disappointed. He released her gaze and looked down at his desk. "You want to it to be real. Real work. Real commitment. Real results."

"Yes. And if that means twenty-four seven, three hundred and sixty-five days a year until we can provide a hundred or more students with the launching pad they need—then that's what it will be." Believing in the program was not her issue. Passion for a cause was what she brought to the table, a fervent desire for success added a crucial element to any enterprise. When desire faded or it didn't need her attention to continue, then it was time to go.

The prince nodded slowly. "Very well...you have the papers with you regarding nonprofit allocations and grant status?"

The shifting gears and the cooler tone unsettled her more. "Yes, but if you are relocating the fund under the Dagmar Foundation, they'll have to be redrafted."

"I am aware." He smiled, but no happiness or pleasure reflected in his eyes. "I will pass those grants to our legal department. They can make the required amendments."

Anna frowned. "I would prefer to handle that myself. Granted, I'll need to be up to speed on the foundation, but the best presentations come from a knowledgeable director. I can highlight the benefits and I'm deep in the drafting of our position papers right now."

He leaned back against the desk, curling his hands against the edge and studying her. "How much do you know about the Dagmar Foundation?"

She swallowed. "Not much, honestly."

"Intriguing. It is one of the largest benefactors in the United States and the European Union. I believe we've provided grants to Hart House on at least three occasions." His mouth tightened, but his voice remained even—deep, husky and compelling. When he added a true smile to that sexy come-hither voice he could rule the world.

"I wasn't aware of that." *Liar.*

He lifted his eyebrows skeptically.

She sighed and dropped her gaze, looking at the carpet near his shoes. The polished wing tips looked uncomfortable and a far cry from the muddy, stained sneakers he raced around campus in. "All right, yes, I was aware of it. I approved the applications for the grants."

"Approved, but you did not write them." *Was that another hint of disappointment?*

"No. *I* didn't. My assistant director believed the Dagmar Foundation's alcoholic recovery program made for a good match, particularly when we added AA meetings and counselors to our different homes in a bid to combat drug and alcohol abuse in the recovering families. All told, I believe the foundation provided four point six million dollars in grants to help us launch."

"And you know this without referring to your notes?" He canted his head to the right, studying her with a fresh gleam of interest. She accepted the attention, refusing to look away.

"I can tell you the dates if you like. I remember when the whales are landed because of the help they provide." Distance. They needed firm boundaries and distance. *Charlie's just the figurehead who signs checks...*

"Interesting analogy." He turned and leaned over to press a button on the desk. "Gretchen, please cancel my appointments for the rest of the week and pencil Miss Novak in."

"Yes, Your Highness. You have the event on Friday..."

Anna opened her mouth to refuse the non-invitation to spend an entire week with him. One hour killed her. She wouldn't survive the week. He frowned at the secretary's response, however, and Anna held her tongue.

"Get me a second ticket. Miss Novak can accompany me."

"Hey..." She crossed her arms. "I have a full schedule this week—"

"And you can amend it. You need to be brought up to speed on the foundation if you plan to redraft those applications and they're due in ten days. So, we have a week to get you everything you need." High-handed and dictatorial manner aside, he wasn't wrong.

It irked her.

"Fine, then set me up with someone in your legal department. I'll have a lot of questions and need specific details that only someone who handles the day-to-day affairs can..." She trailed off, because he smiled. Her heart did a little flip-flop in her chest, because the smile stripped away the years and catapulted her back to when he'd asked her out.

After following her from class to the library to her first job and later her second—every single day for a week—he'd worn down her resistance and always asked with that smile. It disrupted her neurons and turned her into a quivering mass of feminine need. She sucked in a deep breath and shoved the memory away.

"I am the best person for the job. I have been in charge of the foundation for ten years and I've spent the last five as managing director." He pushed away from the desk. "You need the best resources and the best opportunities to make the Alyxandretta scholarship fly. I can give it wings. But...it's your choice."

He circled the desk. "Unfortunately, we can't begin today. So, if you'll see yourself out, I'll expect you at nine a.m. tomorrow. If you're not here, I'll assume the scholarship fund will need a new director. Good day."

Dismissed, she stood there and floundered for a moment. He flipped open his laptop and didn't look at her at all. She moistened her lips and picked up her things. She wanted to say something else, but the words tasted like ash on her tongue.

"Your Highness." It sounded lame to her ears, but it was the best she could manage.

Her hand was on the door handle when he spoke again. "You can call me Charlie, Anna."

Pain eviscerated her and she closed her eyes, grateful he couldn't see her face. "No, Your Highness, I can't. Charlie was a lie, and I would prefer that we keep this professional."

He sighed, but she pulled the door open and strode down the hallway. Security could close it behind her. The art on the walls wavered through the sheen of tears in her eyes. She held it together all the way to the elevator. Once inside, she spared a look at the camera and locked her expression.

*It's all for the kids. I can do this.*

# CHAPTER 2
# ARMAND

Richard circled the billiard's table, eyeing potential shots. "You're one crazy son of a bitch, Armand. What did you think she was going to do? See you again and beg you to take her back?"

Armand said nothing; he stared at the green felt table as though it might reveal the answer.

"Armand, seriously?" His best friend looked up from his shot. "You didn't."

The problem with Richard lay in how well he knew Armand. "I didn't plan on groveling on bended knee." *But yes, I thought she would be more...more her...*

She'd refused to drink out of the bottle, then ignored the glass he'd poured for her.

The attorney angled his hand against the edge of the table, balancing the cue stick between the thumb and forefinger. He snapped the stick forward and it tapped the cue ball, sending it careening after the blue stripe and sinking it. "You're an idiot."

"Helpful." Armand sighed. His body hummed at the memory of her perfume, sweet and exotic. She'd rarely worn any when they lived together, but her shampoo—it had smelled of citrus and orchids, just like she did today.

"Look, I can do a lot, but the fact you even thought she would be happy to see you based on a summons to appear or lose her funding? Where did your diplomacy go?" Richard circled the table and cleared a second ball from the table.

"It's been ten years. I thought—hoped—her temper might have cooled." Ten years to regret leaving him—to regret never calling. When Richard sank a third shot, Armand set the pool cue aside and walked over to the bar. He needed something a lot stronger than water. From the moment she walked into his office, his response swamped his good sense and judgment. He'd wanted to run his fingers through her hair.

She was beautiful—heart-wrenchingly beautiful—but too pale. She'd squinted, as if her head bothered her, and for just the barest of seconds he glimpsed an unsteady step, a waver in her professional façade. He'd caught her arm—he just wanted to help—but she jerked away as if he'd hit her.

Anger had flared in her eyes, a fiery beast if ever there was one. God, but the woman possessed a temper. Why the hell did he arrange to spend the rest of the week with her? She'd clearly wanted to be anywhere except his office. *And the last thing I need is to spend it with her.* But he'd wanted to know if she'd gotten over them—over *him.* Clearly, she had. *So why hang on to something that never had a chance in the first place?*

He poured in three fingers of brandy and tossed the whole thing back. The liquid heat burned through his system, churning his already agitated gut.

"Call Nikole. Get laid. You'll feel better."

"The wisdom of the ancients there, my friend." Armand snorted, ignoring the curl of disgust at the very idea. "Nikole wants a marriage proposal and has informed me that if I wish to enjoy time with her, I must be prepared to put a ring on it."

Richard laughed.

Turning to stare at his friend, he couldn't help his own reluctant smile. "Yes, exactly so." He poured another drink. "Nikole is not the one I want."

"I know." The attorney sobered and finally missed a shot. He joined Armand at the bar and poured his own drink. "So, give yourself a few weeks and pick out another model. You like them, they're easy and you can forget today."

"I'm spending the rest of the week with Anna." He waited for Richard's reaction, and the man didn't disappoint.

He choked, sputtering on the brandy, and swung his gaze up to stare at him. "Why?"

"She will be administrating Alyx's scholarship fund and we're folding it under the Dagmar Foundation. She'll need to be brought up to speed." Any of a dozen executives and administrative staff could handle it

23

"Bullshit." Few people ever spoke to him like that—none while he grew up—and only two in his adulthood. Of those two, only Richard remained. "Since we're on the subject, when were you planning to tell me we were adding that program to the Dagmar Foundation?"

"Tonight. I need the paperwork pushed through by morning." He looked at the amber liquid in the glass and swirled it around. She'd never liked wines or decanted liquors. She preferred beer—in the bottle—the cheaper the better. She liked seven-topping pizzas and sticky caramels mixed in with her popcorn. She'd always tasted of sin and sweetness when they kissed.

Richard snapped his fingers in Armand's face. "Dude, you have it bad."

Shaking off the alluring memories, he took another drink. It would be his last for the night. He would require all his wits about him in the morning if—when—she arrived for their session. "You haven't called me dude in years."

"You haven't been this stupid over a woman in years." The attorney leaned on the bar. "Tell me this—when did you decide to fold in that scholarship?"

Armand didn't answer. The visceral blow he'd experienced when he saw her name in Alyx's email lingered. He couldn't believe it was really her—life and fate were not that cruel. Or so he always believed.

"When, Armand?" Richard repeated the question.

"After I found out Alyx hired her to be in charge of it." He wasn't proud of the admission. He'd spent an hour talking Alyx into placing her scholarship fund under the oversight of the Dagmar Foundation and then promised the newlywed he would handle all the details. The further he put Alyx out of Anna's reach, the more in control he could exert.

"And the goal of this exercise?"

"To provide educational opportunities to underprivileged youth." He drained the brandy and grabbed his pool cue, avoiding Richard's knowing gaze and the truth. He could dance around both for some time. He lined up the shot and sank two balls. He completed two more shots before glancing up. "I want her back."

"Okay." He nodded slowly. "Then we need a plan."

"I've got her attention—well, I commandeered her attention." *If she shows up—if she doesn't just refuse to work with me altogether...*

The attorney pulled out his phone. "So that's step one, what's the next step?"

Armand stared at the shot he lined up and blinked slowly.

"You have a next step—right?" Richard sighed.

No, he'd barely managed to push through that meeting with her today. Bringing her back tomorrow bought him some time.

"This isn't you, Armand. You don't twist in the wind and act all indecisive. What do you want to do next?"

He wanted to pin her against the wall and kiss her senseless. He wanted to lap up all that radiant passion she so easily shared with him. He wanted to find out what movies she liked and what book she curled up in bed with at night. He wanted...

Slamming the pool cue down on the table, he ignored Richard's wince. "I want to know everything about her life. Where is she living? Is she living with someone?" The thought made him sick, but he pressed on. "What does she spend her free time on?"

Richard nodded, his thumbs moving swiftly as he typed on his phone. "And while we dig up all this information?"

He cleared his schedule. Anna was his only talking point. "She hates the title."

"That's resentment, not hate." Richard corrected. "But it's an advantage. Use it."

"To do what? Chase her away again? Let her box me up and put me squarely in the category she believes I belong?" He scowled. For someone so tempestuous and grounded in reality, she maintained a very black-and-white view of the world.

Thirteen years before, a busty little brunette burst into his introduction to business ethics class, interrupted the professor's dry as hell lecture, and set the whole classroom laughing. With few seats to be had in the packed hall, he'd offered her his and she'd made him sit back down, while she squeezed into the narrow space next to him.

Their thighs touched for the entire class.

He never did hear what the professor droned on about with regard to compliance laws. He'd introduced himself, but she barely shook his hand before racing off. He didn't even know what color her eyes were. A bribe at the register's office earned him her schedule, and he'd waited for her outside her next class. The workload surprised him, but a week of putting himself in her path worked.

She'd said yes when he asked her out.

"Where does she jog in the morning? What coffee shop does she frequent? Where does she shop?" He drummed his fingers. "Her address is in the file, get that for me..."

"There's a law against stalking."

"Don't be my attorney, Richard. Be my friend —help me."

"Call her. Make up some excuse and get her on the phone." Richard glanced at his watch. "It's late, but it can't hurt if you're the last thing she thinks about before she goes to sleep."

"Unless she hates me."

"Oh, she's probably angry, and like I said earlier, she resents the title. And the lie." The droll response didn't make him feel better. Richard held up his hands. "Look, you made a mistake and you paid for it—but at the end of the day, *she* was the one who walked."

"She walked away because I'm a prince." The bitter churn of that fact burned.

"You can't change the fact that you're a prince —or I guess you can. But it's not in you to drop

27

the titles altogether and walk away from your family." Richard always knew what buttons to push. Armand was the head of his family, he couldn't—and would never—abandon them.

"You are very good at poking holes, Richard, but do you have any suggestions?" He bit off the next words because his friend didn't deserve the anger. Not this time. If anyone was at fault it was Armand himself.

"You can't stop being a prince, Armand. So why bother?" Richard rolled his sleeves down one at a time and buttoned them at the cuffs. Their billiards game was over.

"What's your point?" They'd already established that his position had an undesirable effect on Anna.

"My point, *Your Highness.*" Richard shrugged on his jacket. Disapproval rang in his words—he only used the appellation when Armand annoyed him. "You can't stop being a prince, so why not use it to your advantage?"

*Use it to my advantage how? She doesn't like the damn title.* He frowned.

Richard pulled his keys out of his pocket. "I'll call you in the morning. I have some strings to go pull so you can stalk—I mean *court*—your lady."

Armand half-scowled, then waved a hand, still considering his friend's advice. He left the pool table as it was—someone would be along to straighten it—and walked through the apartment he maintained in the city. It was a recent acquisition, purchased after the family learned about his cousin's existence. He'd intended to give her the penthouse, but her subsequent marriage to Daniel Voldakov had changed his mind.

Just ten rooms, the penthouse was silent. He maintained a staff but gave them their own apartments downstairs rather than have them live in. Privacy was a rare commodity—rarer still with the increase in security the family endured over recent months thanks to negative publicity in Eastern Europe. Between his cousin Francesca's sudden interest in military service, Rosemary's determination to be in every tabloid and his brother George's behavior, it was a wonder he'd managed the last few months in Los Angeles at all.

In the kitchen, he opened the refrigerator and stared at the labeled containers. The housekeeper hated it when he rummaged, but she wasn't here to stop him so he claimed a random Tupperware container and carried it out to the sunken living room. The city lights gleamed in the darkness beyond the windows of the tower. Stabbing a fork into a piece of shrimp, he ate without tasting the rich sauce he normally favored.

He couldn't get Anna out of his mind.

*"EXACTLY HOW DOES this help me study for my final again?" She sprawled across his chest, her hair clinging to his damp skin.*

*"Stress reliever." He grinned, trailing his fingers up and down her spine. He loved her like this, boneless and loose from sex. "The release of endorphins will help us retain what we're reading."*

29

*Laughter shook her and she lifted her head, a lazy smile curving her lips. "You are so full of it, Charlie. You just wanted to get laid."*

*"Do you feel better?" He traced the curve of her shoulder and the soft line of her throat. She had the most beautiful neck, long and graceful.*

*"Hmm." She closed her eyes and leaned into his gentle caress. "I definitely don't have a headache anymore."*

*"Which will contribute to your ability to study." He might not get any more done, content to simply lie here and touch her.*

*"True." Eyes half-open like a cat about to purr, Anna stretched. The delicious friction of her sweat-slicked body on his roused him all over again. The doorbell rang and his contented kitten popped up. "Food!"*

*Armand groaned, but Anna already bounced to her feet and grabbed his shirt from the clothes they'd stripped off earlier. Fortunately, with his height, the shirt struck her at midthigh.*

*The doorbell rang again and she vanished down the hall. Sitting, he fumbled for his abandoned jeans and dragged them on.*

*"Charlie?"*

*"Anna...?" The strained note in her voice urged him to action. His security knew not to flirt with her, though they still did it occasionally to give him a hard time.*

*Halfway up the hallway, the quiet murmur of multiple male voices penetrated the pleasured haze and he frowned. He halted at the entrance to the* living room—across the narrow space he and Anna called home. Three things struck him at once.

The man in the doorway was Gerard Danielson, the head of his father's private security force. He was framed on either side by two others—Michel Jerome, the family's legal representative in the United States and Peterson, the senior member of Armand's personal security. They were in his doorway. All three men stiffened as he appeared, then bowed.

His heart sank. They'd bowed to him in front of Anna.

"Your Highness," Gerard began without preamble. "Please forgive the lateness of the hour, but this news had to be delivered in person. His Imperial Highness, Grand Duke Phillipe, passed away late yesterday afternoon..."

His father. Dead.

Time stopped.

His university life was over.

"...all announcements were delayed until you could be informed..."

Anna turned a bewildered look in his direction. His world shredded.

"...the plane has been fueled and we have made all security arrangements to bring you home..."

Armand stared into Anna's eyes, their languorous heat frosting over. He held out his hand to her and she came, but hesitance marked her steps. Still, she let him pull her stiff frame to him.

"...if you wish Miss Novak to accompany you, we shall have to make additional arrangements, Your Highness. We await your will." Gerard's sympathy *echoed beneath the protocol, but no amount of sympathy could repair what had been shattered.*

SHOVING that dark memory back into the box where it belonged, he looked at the city. He had her address—did she live in a house on the beach? Did she wake every morning to walk out onto a deck and feel the salty kiss of the dawn? Or was it a tiny little house tucked into a bedroom community with neighbors who knew her name?

Most of the people in their apartment complex at school had known her name. She just had a way of making everyone think she cared about what was going on with them. They reached out, firmed the connection and renewed it with every meeting.

He put the container down and walked over to the phone. He stared at the digits on the receiver. All he had to do was pick it up.

*"You can't stop being a prince, so why not use it to your advantage?"*

He could only think of one person to call, and after another long moment, he picked it up and dialed.

～

ANNA

It was barely five in the morning when her phone rang. Anna thumbed it off and rolled back over. She didn't get up before seven a.m. unless the house was on fire. A minute later her phone pealed out Adele, her sister's ringtone. She shut it off again. When it rang for the third time, she thumbed it on to answer. "*What?*"

"Oh. My. God. How could you start seeing him again and not tell us—scratch that—tell me? How could you not tell *me?* It's so romantic." Penny's voice crackled with excitement. "So, when did it happen? Last month when you had that 'conference' to attend in Milan? Oh, I know, when you were in New York a few months ago and *didn't have time* to see me."

Her sister's voice kept climbing, revving up with excitement, and it pierced the fog of sleep clouding her mind, threatening to ruin the rest of her morning's rest. "Penny. It's five in the morning. I keep telling you that there's a three-hour time difference."

"Holy fuck, are you in bed with him right now?"

The ice pick burrowed into Anna's brain.

"In bed with who? What are you talking about?" Pushing the covers back, Anna sat and grimaced at her sister's whine. Penny was the worst of her siblings when it came to recognizing other people needed sleep. A night owl by nature, she pounced at the worst hours to ask the most ridiculous things.

"You and Charlie—I mean the prince—does he mind if I call him Charlie? I am your sister and if you two are back together that means royal wedding and I can be the next Pippa. Oh God— you think I'll get a spread in *People* magazine?"

Awake now, irritation flared through her. "Penny!"

"Sorry, got a little carried away." Her sister squealed again. "I'm just so happy for you. And for me, because I'm going to look fabulous on television."

"What are you talking about?" And how the hell did her sister know she'd seen the prince the day before? She told no one—least of all her family. They'd been as supportive as they could—her brothers had even threatened to beat him up—but they went through that mourning with her once. She didn't want to open old wounds.

"You getting back together with Charlie, it's so romantic."

Her blood went cold. "I am not—we're *not* together."

"Oh yes you are, it's all over ACE this morning. 'Playboy Prince reunites with his first love.' I still can't believe you didn't *tell* me..." Her sister continued to yammer, but Anna fumbled for the television remote and turned it on. She found the ACE channel by scanning the guide and stared. A commercial offering superstar figures detailed how every woman could look like a model segued into a red-dressed studio where the reporter started talking.

Thumbing up the volume, she waited.

"...and recapping our top of the hour, playboy prince, Armand Dagmar, the titular head of the Andraste royal family, is very well-known for his exotic tastes and revolving door of beauties to grace his arm, but has happily ever after finally rubbed off on him?" Images of Armand cavorting with some blonde model in Majorca punctuated the story. "The grand duke has been seen out and about in the Los Angeles area for months following the fairy-tale reunion with his long-lost cousin, the Princess Alyxandretta. But now sources close to the prince confirm that it wasn't his cousin that kept him in the City of Angels but the chance to recapture romance with his first love, a woman ACE has identified as Anna Novak..." And then her face was on the screen.

"See!" Penny's voice squealed through the phone.

*I'm going to kill him.*

# CHAPTER 3
## ANNA

B y eight a.m. there was a circus parked in front of her little two-bedroom bunga-low. Give the paparazzi a bone and they make a meal out of it. She sipped her coffee, staring at the sea of cameras setting up house-keeping on her lawn. Her poor neighbors gawked at the vans sitting crookedly against the curbs. To leave, she would have to push through them to get to her car.

But they were in her driveway too.

Three took off with her trash. *I hope they like microwavable meal remains and takeout boxes.*

Yesterday's headache returned with a vengeance. When her phones wouldn't stop ring-ing, she took the landline off the hook and shut her cell down. There was no sense in wondering how they got her private number. She did far too much business via her phone. To leave, she had to make them move their cars. But that required she step outside and confront them, then they could just as easily follow her. She wasn't sure how murder would play on national television, so she kept herself planted in the house. Maybe she could hold out two to three days on the coffee and nukables in the freezer.

A pair of black sedans and one SUV pulled right down the center of her already overcrowded street. They prowled like bears lumbering through the woods—and the reporters paid attention.

None of the vehicles parked. Doors opened on the sedan in the lead and two men in black suits with black ties exited.

*Check that—two* huge *men in black suits.* They shouldered their way through the crowd, ignoring the reporters asking them questions. Two more men exited the rear sedan and joined the first. Three took charge of the crowd, backing them off her lawn and right down to the sidewalk. Walking tanks had that effect.

The fourth man walked right up on her porch and rang the doorbell. Once.

She checked the peephole. Just the single man standing on her porch, the crowd of reporters pushed back—but she knew long-range cameras. They didn't have to be in her face to get a picture.

Deciding against opening the door, she slid sideways and pressed her ear to the wood. "Yes?"

"Miss Novak, His Highness sent us to provide you with a safe escort to the Petersburg Tower." She heard the deep baritone clearly despite the door's muffling effects.

She cut off the knee-jerk reaction to ask the

security guard to tell his boss to go to hell. Taking her temper out on him would serve no purpose. She'd rather smack His Highness personally.

"Give me a few minutes, please." The amazing calm in her voice impressed her—the rage trembling inside her defied description.

"Take your time, Miss Novak."

She glanced back out the peephole but only saw the back of the man's suit coat. She cleaned up her coffee cup in the kitchen, shut off the pot and emptied it as well. She took her time wiping down the counters and setting up the coffeemaker for another brew later. In her bedroom, she surveyed her clothes and chose her most professional business outfits—slacks, a waistcoat and a periwinkle-blue blouse.

Thankfully, she'd showered for after hanging up on her sister. She used a flat iron to straighten her hair, methodically putting herself together. His Imperial Highness may have sent in his private security as troops, but she wasn't some impressionable coed. And she sure as hell didn't think flooding her with peeping toms was a way to win friends and influence people.

She used the bare minimum of cosmetics.

This wasn't a date. She geared up for battle.

Straightening up the bathroom, she had no more excuses to make the security guards wait. She packed her workbag and her laptop. She still had the scholarship papers in her bag from the day before. She paused in the second bedroom and picked up a small filing box. It contained the hard-copy application for federal grant money.

They could work off the soft copy on her laptop, but she wanted to be prepared for everything.

Sunglasses in place and keys in hand, she slid her purse strap onto her shoulder and carried both bags to the door. She knocked on it once before turning the security locks—all four of them.

"One moment, ma'am." Sculpted politeness kept the words from being an order.

She waited as he requested. It couldn't have been more than a minute when the door opened and the guard filled the partial space he allowed. He glanced at her and then offered a hand. "Would you like me to carry those?"

Surrendering the file case, she held on to her laptop bag. "Thank you."

"Walk straight for the SUV in the center. We'll be right with you all the way. Don't engage. Don't meet their gazes. Smile if you feel like it, but otherwise just walk like you do this every day." He gave her a quick, tight smile. "Fortunately, it's only the press. Keys?"

*Fortunately? Odd word choice.* She kept her comments to herself and handed him the door keys. She appreciated the advice. He stepped back and opened the door farther. The two additional men in black suits stood at the edge of the porch, shoulder to shoulder. The crowd stirred as she walked out. She glanced back at the first security guard, but he waved her on.

"I'll lock up."

"Okay." Steeling herself with a deep breath

she followed the men in front of her. Camera shutters clicked, questions tossed out.

*"When did you and the prince meet?"*

*"Has he asked you to marry him?"*

*"Were you introduced by the princess?"*

*"Anna! Over here!"*

*"Are you working together?"*

*"Do you think the family should be restored?"*

*"Will you wear a crown?"*

*"Anna! Look this way!"*

*"What's your favorite color?"*

She walked straight for the SUV. The men in front of her didn't let anyone get close. The three on the side created a barricade to step through the throng, into the street, between the cars and to the open back door of the Escalade.

A siren whooped-whooped down the street, blue-and-reds flashing, and reporters scrambled for their vehicles. Three were stopped by the police officers. Glancing back once, she zeroed her attention on the dozen or so cameras pointed in her direction.

Security closed the door, insulating her from the sound. The man from her door slid into the front passenger seat. Another tapped the roof of the car. The sedan in front of them pulled away and they quickly followed.

Twisting, Anna watched the other sedan continue to block the road—hampering the press's attempt to follow her. Exhaling, she leaned back and crossed one leg over the other.

"Go ahead and put your seatbelt on, Miss Novak." The man from her front door instructed over his shoulder.

"I'm sorry, I didn't catch your name earlier." The steadiness of her voice didn't translate to her fingers. They trembled and she fumbled with the seat belt.

"Johnson. Kyle Johnson." He glanced back and gave her another quick smile. "It's nice to meet you, ma'am."

"Thank you, Mr. Johnson. I wasn't entirely sure how I was going to get out of there."

"Not a problem. We'll have you at the tower soon. It's secure and they won't be able to follow you inside."

"Fantastic." The sarcasm escaped before she could bottle it. She folded her hands together and turned her gaze to the passing streets. Los Angeles traffic was never pleasant, but they didn't approach the highways. It probably made sense to them. The last place she wanted to be headed was the tower. Armand was there. Her stomach bottomed out, and she forced her focus back onto their route. She recognized the bypass—they were swinging wide of the city and coming back in from the south.

A phone rang, but hers was still buried in her purse—off.

Kyle answered.

"Yes, sir. She's secure." He glanced back at her. "His Highness says he has been calling your phone."

"It's off." She didn't look at him.

"She turned her cell phone off, sir...yes, sir...

one moment please, sir." Kyle extended the phone to her. "His Highness would like a word, Miss Novak."

She stared at the phone.

It wouldn't be fair to Kyle to refuse and make him explain it to his employer.

Accepting the phone, she studied the screen and hit the off button. She passed the phone back to Kyle. "Thank you."

The man's impassive expression didn't shift as he took it back. He looked at the blank screen and waited. Sure enough, it rang again. "Hello, sir."

The silence in the front stretched and Anna made herself look out the window again. She refused to let the mask slip. Anger could sustain her, because no way would she arrive with swollen eyes and a red nose. She'd shed enough tears for him. They wound through the downtown canyon of skyscrapers toward the bright blue-glassed tower destination.

"No, sir, I handed her the phone. Yes, she hung up, sir." Poor Kyle kept his tone placid and even. He might as well have been discussing the weather.

A niggle of guilt wormed its way through her anger.

"Miss Novak, His Highness has asked me to request a moment of your time to speak to him on the phone without hanging up."

She glanced back at the security guard and sighed. She held out her hand and he passed her the phone. She put it to her ear. "Yes, *Your Highness?*"

"Anna." Armand's voice lowered, and the accent wrapped around her name like a caress. But she fought the fluttering response in her belly. "Are you alright?"

"I'm fine. And you?" Polite. Perfunctory. Perfect. She congratulated herself.

He sighed. "You will be here soon and we can discuss how to handle this."

"We have a meeting at nine, Your Highness, to discuss the scholarship fund." And that was all. Even with the outrage and fury armoring her bruised heart, his concern managed to find a chink. She needed to shore that up.

Now.

"Yes, but this is a little more pressing—"

She cut him off. "If by pressing you mean annoying, invasive, and stretching the boundaries of credulity, then you would be absolutely correct. Goodbye, Your Highness." She shut the phone off and set it down on the seat next to her. It rang again. The number identified Tower One and she looked at Kyle. "Will you get in trouble if *I* ignore it?"

"No, ma'am." One corner of his mouth quirked, but she didn't know him well enough to identify it as a real smile or not.

She declined the call.

It rang again. She hit the ignore button again.

She repeated the process four more times before they arrived at the tower and drove down into a parking garage. A private gate rolled open and the standing security waved them through. The shadowy garage blocked out the morning brightness and she pushed up her sunglasses with reluctance. She preferred the shield they provided, but she could hardly get away with them indoors.

They parked next to a bank of elevators and two more plainclothes security guards stood at either end. Uneasiness spread through her. When she arrived at the Petersburg Tower the day before, she'd passed through a relatively normal level of security scrutiny, but this seemed over the top.

Kyle exited first, then opened her door.

"Is something else going on?" She stepped out and frowned. Even in the deep recess of the parking garage, the men ranged out around her and she had only a few feet to cross into the waiting elevator.

"Nothing to worry about, Miss Novak." Kyle gave her a polite, if encouraging, smile and gestured to the elevator. He held her file box in one hand and she returned his phone to him before she picked up her laptop bag. Inside, he inserted a key and pressed a button and the doors closed and they swooped upward.

At the top, the doors opened onto a cream-colored hallway.

No security guards in sight.

Kyle braced the doors to let her exit. He led her down the hall to the only door and knocked.

It swung inward and the Grand Duke Armand Dagmar waited—dressed in a blue button-down sans jacket and tie. Unlike the day before, his tidy hair fell in a sway toward his eyes. Her fingers itched to comb it back where it belonged. His tight expression eased when he looked at her, then he reached out to take the case from Kyle.

"Thank you, Johnson."

"Of course, sir."

Belatedly she realized Kyle's job was over. He would leave her alone with the prince.

Oddly disappointed, she summoned a smile. "Thank you, Kyle."

"My pleasure, Miss Novak. When you're ready to go, just ring down and we'll have your car ready." That sounded odd, particularly since her car remained parked in the garage at her house, but she let it go.

Her gaze collided with Armand's and they stood there, silently, until the elevator closed behind Kyle.

"Come in...please?" He seemed to tack that word on as an afterthought.

She stepped around him and into...his apartment. The gorgeous suite couldn't be anything else—from the sunken living room and ninety-inch flat-screen television to the bank of windows offering an even better view of the city than his office possessed. She hadn't realized he actually lived in the tower—but the European aristocrat must need someplace to call home.

"May I take your jacket?" His hands touched her shoulders lightly and she forced herself not to flinch.

"No. You *may* not." Forging ahead, she walked

over to a table set up in the corner and set her bags down. Stripping off her own jacket, she hung it on the back of a chair, then went to work setting up her files.

"Anna..."

"I am here to do my job, Your Highness. If you don't want to work, I can ring down for Kyle and leave." Her voice didn't quiver once.

"Anna." He scowled, irritation darkening his tone. He hated to repeat himself. Charlie was never calm or collected. He laughed out loud, he argued with fervor, made love with vigor, and even yelled when the occasion warranted it.

*Dammit, he's not Charlie and he never was.*

"Don't you dare *Anna* me. Sources close to the prince? The only source close enough to you to spout that line of drivel is Rick and he was never an ass hat and never ratted out your secrets. So who the else do you suppose is to blame?"

*Okay, so much for calm.*

❧

## ARMAND

He deserved the fiery lash of her temper. He'd expected it from the moment she walked in—but no, a cold, detached zombie breezed into his apartment, leaving an icy chill in her wake. "You just assume *I* called and put the press up to that?"

"Didn't you?" she fired back, the heat in her glare scorching him despite the distance between them. "Or do you think your curtsying secretary

47

did it? Oh, I know, the hot dog vendor on the corner recognized me from our college days and put one and two together to come up with sixty-nine."

The tension fisting around his gut since he woke that morning eased. His Anna still lurked beneath the rigid surface, boiling like a volcano threatening eruption. "*No one* in my office would have released your name."

"No one would release my name—genius. So you call a celebrity gossip station, feed them some cock-and-bull story about romantic re-union to do what?" She stormed toward him, her scent wrapping around him. "Did you have some scandal to clean up? Your brother take up racing again? One too many parties with the sheiks in the Mediterranean? That model Nikole not doing it for you anymore? Or maybe you just wanted to put me in my place?"

"You have never been in your place." He dipped his chin down, capturing her gaze and staring into those gorgeous eyes. It didn't matter that they burned with dislike and threatened to roast him on a spit. Her nearness relaxed the fear squeezing his heart since the news broke. Sum-moning her so peremptorily to his office hadn't been about feeding her to the wolves, but a rash desire to see her again. The type of impulse he'd not allowed himself since she walked away from him.

"Why, Ch—" She coughed, seemed to catch herself and let out a long breath. "Who, then, *Your Highness?* Who would do that?"

"No." Armand shook his head slowly. Her anger—her righteous rage—flooded color into her cheeks. The ice thawed.

That took her aback. "I'm sorry, what?"

"No. Not 'Your Highness.' You want to ask me questions and speak to me like that, then you use my name." He pivoted and walked over to the coffee service the housekeeper set out. "Coffee, before we begin?"

She said nothing.

He allowed her to digest the comment.

"Your Highness?"

And got heartburn for his trouble. "Yes, Miss Novak?"

"I think you owe me an explanation." The censure in her words overrode the mild tone.

*Do I really? Or do you simply want one?* He studied her over the mug of coffee, taking his time to sip. She was here. She was safe. He could afford to let this play out. "I think you owe me the courtesy of addressing me by my name."

"Courtesy?" The three syllables climbed one-half note each. The color of her lips seemed to darken against the rosy complexion and her eyes sparked. If she hadn't forced her hair to tame with some straightening iron, she'd be the image of a fiery Celtic goddess.

He couldn't help the grin the mental image produced. "Yes, a politeness shown to strangers and friends alike—" he walked toward her as he spoke, setting the coffee cup down on the table. To his immense pleasure, she didn't back away,

"—and I want you to remember just how well we know each other."

Her kissable lips pursed and he leaned in, the sweet scent of her shampoo and soap arousing far sweeter memories—but a hand slapped against his chest. He froze. She touched him. Palm flat against his shirt. Her fingers seemed to burn right through the fabric, imprinting on his skin. His heart slammed against his ribs, as eager as a dog on a chain to leap free.

"You're an ass." She gave him a shove, but it did little other than to push herself back a few inches. She started to circle him and he caught her arm, missing the feeling of her hand on his chest already.

"Say my name, Anna." He spun her around—boxed her against the table, planting his body close enough that his thighs brushed hers and her chest pushed up against his with every breath. This close, she had to tilt her head back to look at him. Without the heels, she stood six inches shorter than he, but even in them she was not a match for his height.

"Stop it." The order bounced off his temper—he ignored it.

He allowed himself the singular pleasure of running a finger down her cheek. She didn't flinch, but her swift inhale of breath gave him enormous satisfaction. She wasn't as immune—or as over him—as she pretended. "Sweet Anna, you can tell me whatever you want—order me around, fight with me, get angry, yell—*whatever* you want. When you call my name. Until then..."

It killed him—absolutely killed him—but he leaned close, her body pressed fully up to his. Her lips parted and the pupils of her eyes dilated. He traced his knuckles down her spine and along the curve of her hip, then reached past her to press the button on the intercom. "Gentlemen, we're ready for you now."

Stepping away, he reclaimed his coffee cup and walked to the head of the table. The front door of the penthouse opened, his security admitting Richard and three others from the legal team to help them work through the papers.

He spared a sidelong look at Anna. She struggled to resume her icy reserve, but it was too late.

The passion they shared still flamed beneath the surface. Richard blocked his view when he paused to give her a quick half hug. Jealousy dug its claws into his spine, saved only by her less than lukewarm response to the awkward contact.

"If you will all take your seats." He leaned back in the chair, determined to see this farce through. "Miss Novak needs to be brought up to speed."

She chose the chair farthest away from him, but he contented himself with watching her—for now. His phone buzzed as Richard opened with a quick sketch of the Dagmar Foundation. The message was from his head of security.

They already had a threat.

*Dammit.*

# CHAPTER 4
# ARMAND

" I hope you know what the hell you're doing." Richard said quietly, though Anna was still engrossed with the other attorneys, going over some of the finer points in the initial grant papers. Armand had abandoned the meeting about halfway through to review the threat with Peterson. His security chief deemed it credible, and it followed the same pattern as the others they'd received in the last six months.

"That makes two of us." He'd stopped drinking coffee two hours before—the jittery restlessness in his blood had nothing to do with caffeine. "How bad is it?"

"Bad." Richard kept his back to the others, but he didn't bother to disguise the censure in his tone "What were you thinking?"

"Why do you and she both assume I told the reporter?" It was a disgruntled complaint, but he gave his best friend a dour look anyway.

"Because we're not idiots. There wasn't even a sniff of this in the gossip columns before this

53

morning—and you hadn't set eyes on her—physically—in ten years. Then, the day *after* you invite her to your office and have me jump through legal hoops to get the scholarship fund reallocated, she is suddenly the scoop of the year? Yeah—it's a fair question."

Armand sighed, his gaze on Anna. She studiously avoided looking at him. In fact, she'd ignored him throughout the meeting—answering and asking questions of everyone save him. Fortunately, her tone also chilled when she addressed Richard.

At least he wasn't alone in exile.

"You said use being a prince to my advantage. But I didn't do this. I wouldn't." And when he got his hands on the person who gave her name to the press... His only regret lay in the fact he couldn't order a head to roll.

"Well, this is *not* an advantage, in case you were wondering." Despite his dry humor, Richard didn't bother to disguise his low opinion—one of the reasons their friendship withstood the test of time, distance and press coverage. They fell into a rhythm during their freshman year and they stayed there.

Still, the fracas had given him an opportunity. "Rick, I'm furious about the press, but it doesn't change the fact I wanted to see her—"

"Eh, you've seen her." Richard's brows climbed. "And seeing her dumped her ass right into the fire before she even made it to the frying pan. She's been served her up like so much chum to the sharks. They're going to trot out every

SOME LIKE IT SCANDALOUS

single affair you've ever had. They are going to publicly compare her to every woman they think you've had in your bed. No, my friend, this is a cluster fuck and a half. If she doesn't geld you before this is over, I'll be surprised."

"Whose side are you on?" Irritation scraped over his nerves.

"Yours. But this is a mess, Armand." Richard sighed.

"I'm aware of that fact." Violently aware. No one had to tell him how bad the situation could be. The press smelled scandal—and they had her name. The leak had already produced one threat. "But she reacted—she was angry and she wasn't cold. For a minute there...it was like we were *us* again." *She mentioned Nikole. She knew about her —which means she paid attention.*

Maybe it was petty to hope for a little jealousy. It meant she cared—on some level she still cared. *Or maybe they already highlighted Nikole on the news this morning.*

He ignored the snide mental voice taunting him.

"Pissing her off is not going to get you back into her bed." Richard poured a couple of drinks and glanced over at the table. The others wrapped it up, rising and shaking Anna's hand one at a time. "You have to tell her, you know."

"I know." Impatient at the advice, he blew out a breath. The last thing he wanted to do was scare her.

"All right, we're going to get out of here. Call me if you need someone to punch you out of another bad idea." He pressed the drinks into Armand's hands. "Do both of you a favor, and give her this before you tell her. It might dull the shock."

Richard strode across the room and ushered the others out. Anna didn't spare him more than a polite nod. When the door closed, Armand walked over and held the drink out to her.

She shot him a doubtful look. "It's barely lunchtime. A little early for that, don't you think?"

"No. We need to talk."

"I think we've said enough today, *Your Highness*." She continued packing her papers back into the briefcase. "I also think I have enough to complete the grant application—so we won't need the whole week."

"Anna. I screwed up. I did something stupid and impulsive and now you're coping with the backlash from that. I'm sorry." Endangering her had never been his intention, he'd simply wanted to see her again.

She went still. He worried for a moment that she hadn't heard him. "Thank you." She swallowed. "And—it's okay. It will blow over."

Her easy acceptance startled him. "No. That's why I am sorry—it won't be as easy as that."

"Your—" Her lips compressed and she blew out a breath. "Armand, it'll be fine. Sure they're hungry for a story now, but if we don't give them anything more, it will go away. I've seen you do it any number of times over the years."

Warmth bloomed in his chest. She'd watched

him, kept up with him over the years. He wanted to hold on to that thought before regret and reality crashed in on them.

And she'd said his name.

"This is different." He set the drinks down on the table and put his hands on the back of a chair. "You're different."

"Yeah, I'm not actually sleeping with you." She straightened another set of papers, started to slide them in the case. "Do you want a copy of these notes?"

Her hands trembled, but she moved another stack of papers to the side and wiped a palm against her slacks. He made her nervous. He let go of the chair—laid a hand over hers. "Anna...I need you to listen to me."

She didn't jerk away.

Small step, but he would take it.

"I am listening to you. I can walk and chew gum at the same time." She gave his hand a light smack and he let her go, the gesture so familiar it made his heart hurt. No one ever slapped his hands—not like she did.

Powering down her laptop and packing it was her last step. He waited until she was done, enjoying watching her. Tucking an errant strand of hair behind her ear, she looked up at him. "I'm still listening, but you're not saying anything."

"What would you say if I asked you to stay here in the penthouse—for a few days?" He hedged his bets. Maybe she would agree.

*And maybe purple porcines will stand up and claim the world for Orwell.*

"I'd ask you what year you thought it was." The droll response was so her, he couldn't help but smile. Unfortunately, none of this was funny.

"I know it's only been a few hours since the story broke, but... My security intercepted a very credible threat. It's become something of a problem in the past few months for the family." He could broach the most difficult of topics with oil barons, kings, and presidents—why did he struggle so when talking to her?

"I'm sorry to hear that." The kindness in her expression spoke volumes about her character. She may not even be aware of just how rare it was to feel compassion amid outrage and anger— anger he wholly deserved. "But I hardly see why that leads to that invitation."

"It's not an invitation." He braced himself for the oncoming storm. She would not like his next words. "In fact, that was a polite way of telling you that you need to stay here for a few days. The tower is very secure. We have security in the lobby, in the parking garage and on three floors below us. No one comes up to this level without security in attendance—"

She held up a palm. "You're babbling. I un- derstand the security. I saw them and appreci- ated you sending your men to pick me up. But I'm *not* staying here."

"Yes. You are." He circled the table and caught her before she could pull away from him. She curled her hands into little fists, but he held them gently. "Anna, the threats against my family have increased in the last few months. This morning we received one for you."

"I'm sorry, what?" She blinked. "What are you talking about?"

Armand sighed. He wanted to keep holding her hands, forget the ugly reality that had become his life and tug her over to the sofa and sit down. He wanted to pull her in his lap and interrogate her. Hear about the last ten years—talk like they used to. He wanted that and more—but not at the cost of a knife to her throat.

"Sit down? Talk to me awhile and I will explain everything, I promise."

"No. No." She pulled away from him. "Look, this is an impossible situation and I've tried to be professional and mature and adult. But you're taking this too far—we're *not* together. We're not getting back together and ACE can chat it up all they like, but the difference between fantasy and reality is that happily ever after exists in novels and this is not one."

Easing her into this wasn't an option. "Five."

She blinked. "Five what?"

"Five attempts. In the last six months, there have been five assassination attempts on members of the immediate family. Two car bombings, one aborted shooting and a poisoning."

All the color in her cheeks fled. "That's four…"

"The fifth was a little more personal. A knife attack. Sebastian is still recovering."

Her mouth opened, but no words came out. She sat abruptly and he pulled out a chair, turning it so he could sit facing her.

"How close?" She swallowed. "You said you and your family—how many of those were you? And why hasn't it been in the news?"

"Security keeps events like these quiet. It prevents copycat attacks for news coverage. I wouldn't even tell you—because it shouldn't have affected you until I was a complete idiot. And for that you have my deepest, most profound apologies. I wanted... Well, it doesn't matter what I wanted. I didn't intend for our meeting to become gossip fodder and it leaked anyway." He botched this whole thing. Richard was right to call him an idiot. The press watched every single move he'd made—particularly after Alyx's arrival on the scene.

"I'm sorry that I've drawn more attention to you in Los Angeles." Was she seriously apologizing for *his* mistake?

Releasing one hand, he raked his fingers through his hair. "Anna, this morning's threat was against *you*."

"That's ridiculous—I'm not a member of your family and..." She blinked slowly and leaned back in the chair, pulling free of him. "The story broke this morning. And you got a threat about me this morning. Isn't that a little convenient, Your Highness?"

"Convenient? Not at all. Terrifying? Absolutely. I painted a target on you by demanding you meet with me and until I can get that target off, I need you to be here where we can protect you." He reached for his drink and tossed it back.

She snorted. "This isn't a very funny joke."

"It's not a joke." He didn't want to have to show her the threat, but if that was what it took to convince her... One selfish, stupidly impulsive moment and he put her right in the crosshairs. He should have left her alone.

"You're being ridiculous." She didn't believe him. Why should she? In walking away, she'd never been subjected to his life—his real one. Rising, he picked up his phone and sent a text to Peterson. Anna said nothing as he paced away from her. One minute stretched into three... A knock at the door announced his security chief's arrival.

"Your Highness, Miss Novak." Entering without formality, Peterson crossed the room to set a folder down on the table. "These were sent from an email address that has since been shut down. All IP traces have proven unsuccessful so far."

He set out the first note—a printout with a very direct message.

*Anna Novak made the wrong choice. The Andraste name must die with this generation, it has lived on too long.*

The signature—a coffin draped in his family's royal coat of arms—had left him cold. The words, the boldness of the threat to include Anna, stoked the fury in his soul.

"It's a note that's kind of vague." Despite the lightness of her words, Anna had gone pale as she read. "And you said it came from a spoofed email address—maybe it's a prank."

Peterson glanced at him, seeking his permis-

61

sion to continue. Armand nodded. She had to understand it wasn't a joke, it wasn't some foolish trick or desperate attempt to get attention.

The person or persons behind the escalating threats had delivered on every single one they had sent.

Flipping over the sheet of paper with the note, Peterson revealed three photographs. He set them out on the table one at a time.

They were all of Anna. The third one, Armand had recognized immediately—it showed her leaving the tower the day before, her expression cool and her eyes fierce.

Anna stood and looked down at the pictures. "This one was yesterday." But the third photo didn't hold her attention—it was the first two. The same two that twisted Armand up inside. "These are from college..."

"They know who you are, Anna." He had no idea how they'd found those two pictures, but the timing was too tight. Too close. They had to have them from research or another source. The value in the clue also highlighted the very real threat.

"Miss Novak, we've received threats like these before. They don't have to be specific to be interpreted for the danger they are. Someone, or several someones, want the family line to end. The renewed acquaintance between you and His Highness poses a threat to these individuals. We deem it a *very* credible threat." Peterson had held back the final photo.

"So the gossip channel was already talking

about us, whoever these people are probably got the pictures from some anonymous source at the school..." She grasped at straws.

As much as he would like to leave her peace of mind intact, he had to make her understand.

"Peterson, leave us." He would handle the last photo without an audience. The man left without another word.

Anna frowned, the line between her eyes going tight. That she had a headache didn't surprise him.

He gathered together the photos and the note and put them back into the first folder. Flipping open the second, he slid it across to her.

The photo had been taken from inside her house, while she was asleep in her bed.

Her knees gave out. Armand caught her and helped her into the chair. "Breathe," he ordered, cupping the back of her neck and rubbing his thumb over the wild beat of her pulse. "Breathe."

"They were in my house..." The words came out in a rush.

"I know." Fury bloomed anew in his chest. They'd been in the same room with her while she'd been alone, asleep, and vulnerable.

It was unacceptable to every part of him.

"I can't believe this." She pressed her hands together in front of her face and laughed a sound so hollow it bordered on sadness. "I mean, I take a job working on a scholarship fund and now my name is tabloid fodder and I have a death threat and a stalker. Wow. Have I mentioned just how not good it is to see you again?"

The verbal jab went straight to his heart. "I'm sorry, Anna. Let me try to fix this. I *will* fix this."

"And do what? Make an announcement? Tell everyone no, we're not together? I wasn't born yesterday. I know that the more you feed the press a denial—especially a denial—it will just make them hungrier." It was her turn to rub her face and her eyes gleamed with suspicious dampness, twisting the knife further in his heart. "I can't believe this."

"I know." If only regret could change the past—well, if it could do that, neither of them would be sitting here right now.

Her gaze returned to the last image, again and again, until Armand flipped the folder closed. But she hadn't pulled away from him, and he continued to massage her neck. The taut bunch of her muscles loosened with each caress.

How desperately he wanted to make it all go away. If he could take back that meeting— *God, I would. I wanted to see her again, but not like this.* He glanced at the glass he'd poured for her. "Do you want that drink now?"

She followed his look, then stood before he could and picked it up. She tossed it back with the same fervor he had. He smiled a little. She licked her lips and his brain locked on the action. "I can't stay here, that's the same as admitting to the press that their information on your indiscretion has some basis in fact."

"I don't really give a damn what the press has to say on the subject." The truth of their predicament seemed to be eluding her. "They can speculate I sleep with sheep. It's the threat against you that's the problem."

"But if the press lets it go..." She was reaching and he wanted to let her hold on to that naïve idea.

He really did.

"Fanatics don't care about press reports unless it reinforces their beliefs. You're a target because *I* care and I can lie myself blue in the face to the press, but the simple fact is, if anything happened to you, I wouldn't forgive myself. So you can hate me and you can be angry with me... Until we sort this out, you are staying here, Anna, and end of discussion."

She sank back onto the chair. "So speaks the prince royal—"

Dammit. He'd had more than enough of *that* attitude. Letting go of his patience, he grabbed her chair and jerked it toward him, launching her forward into his arms. His mouth slanted across hers and their lips fused. She came to rest against his chest, half on his lap, with his legs bracketing hers. She froze, but when he massaged her lips, her mouth opened. Her fingers curled against the fabric. Then she kissed him back, her tongue tangling with his, and he was home.

The last light of reason went out in his head.

# CHAPTER 5
## ANNA

er breath hitched in her throat. He grabbed her chair and jerked her forward. She all but fell against his chest, the last thing she saw was the anger flaming in her eyes. Her protest died unspoken when he dipped his head and claimed her mouth. She planted her hands on his chest, intending to shove him away, but her fingers curled into the fabric of his shirt, her anger dissolving beneath the passion in his kiss.

*This is Charlie...*

The thought floated, disconnected, above the surge of emotion. Her blood went hot, blazing through the wild fever of her temper. Irritation—with herself, with him, with the whole damn situation—melted under the assault of his lips. But no matter the quiet fury in his eyes, his kiss was gentle, possessive, and utterly disarming. His lips glided over hers—tentative, remembering—and when her mouth opened, his tongue slid into stroke against hers.

Oh God. No one tasted as good as Charlie did. Nothing battered right through the years of hurt, regret, and loneliness like the soft, wet kiss of his lips and the warm glide of his hands slipping down her body. She wasn't in the chair anymore. He dragged her across until she sat on his lap, lost in the sweet surrender of being close to him.

He sucked on her tongue and heat unfurled like a great sail snapping open to catch the wild wind. Her heart beat so fast it had to be trying to escape. When he released her lips to kiss down the side of her neck, she moaned.

The essence of them—the quick passion, the fury of it taking them—it was all there. It didn't matter who reached for whom, or where they were. The world disintegrated, falling away to leave only them. His teeth grazed the pulse point in her throat and she slid her hands up into that dark tumble of hair. Soft and silky—just like she remembered it. Memory and reality crashed together, dragging her beneath the riptide.

Her nipples strained against the bra, the fabric rasping against their sensitive tips. Dear God, she wanted him. She needed him. She'd told herself for ten years she didn't—she lied to herself and let the lie keep her warm at night, but the icy chill of their long separation exploded. She dug her nails in, impatient with their clothes.

He pulled away and nudged her back to her own chair.

It was so fast, her head spun, and she couldn't catch her breath. She opened her eyes and tried to hold on to him, but he left her, shoving his chair back and rising before she could catch his hands. His eyes were black—the pupil having swallowed the iris—and they were intense with desire.

"Charlie..."

He shook his head and circled away from the table, raking his fingers through disheveled hair. "My apologies—I didn't mean to maul you that way."

Why wouldn't he look at her?

"Please, stay here. Security has orders to keep you in the building if necessary." His husky voice betrayed no quiver. "I'll—excuse me. I'll be with you in a few moments."

And then he was gone.

Touching two fingers to her lips, she stifled the scream of frustration welling up. What the hell had she been thinking? She'd spent the whole morning fuming mad at him—then one kiss and she was ready to get naked?

*I am in so much trouble...*

"IF YOU'RE NOT TOGETHER, why are you staying in his penthouse?" Penny demanded over the phone. Anna should never have told her little sister that she would be staying with Armand. For that matter, she shouldn't have agreed at all. Particularly since his few minutes turned into hours—he simply didn't return. She sat at the table like an idiot for over forty-five minutes. When she went in search of him, she'd discovered he'd left the apartment through another entrance.

One guarded by security.

They'd ushered her back inside and requested that she wait for the prince to return.

Six hours later, waitstaff entered, prepared a meal, then served it and he still wasn't back. He might have inflamed her passion, but he pissed her off even more. The housekeeper showed her to a room and now she sat—still waiting for him.

"Look, Penny—it's just for a couple of days until they get this nonsense with the press sorted out." The explanation sounded even lamer out loud than it did in her head. No way in hell would she tell her baby sister about the threats. Not when icy terror slithered through her each time she considered the last picture. Whoever *they* were, they'd been in her room.

"Because moving in with him will show those guys just how wrong they got the story?" Penny snorted. "Is it nice? As nice as that palace they have in Norway?"

"It's a penthouse. Of course it's nice. But it's also empty." Not that his apartment wasn't decorated—but the decorations were impersonal right down to the knickknacks. No photos of family, not even any paintings or works from Charlie's favorites. She sighed. She had to stop thinking of him as Charlie.

Charlie was the lie, Armand the reality.

*Accept it—you don't want the prince; you want your boyfriend back.*

"So, is he there? Like right now?" Her sister's

enthusiasm seemed to have diminished during the day.

"No. He went out." She didn't mention the kiss or the raging passion that left her restless and aching all day.

"Bummer."

"If you say so." She tried for glib and light, but exhaustion warred with need—she wanted him to come home. Then she could yell at him for walking away. Yes, that was what she wanted.

"Anna, are you really okay with all of this? I mean if you're not really back together..." Bless her heart, give her sister a little while to bask in the pseudo-royal glory and she still returned to earth.

"No." She didn't lie this time. "No, I'm not all right. But I will be. Just avoid the press, okay? Don't go for the Pippa thing. Mom texted me that they had to call the police to shoo them off the lawn."

"I won't. I mean...it would be fun and all. But only if you were happy."

"I love you too, kiddo."

"I know, I'm fabulous. And there's Billy. We're off to the village tonight, new bands playing. Love you."

"Love you." Then her sister was gone, her mood ping-ponging from sympathetic and loving to excited for her next adventure. The eight years separating them seemed vast more often than not, but Penny was good people. Thankfully, Anna's phone had stopped ringing nonstop when she switched the cell back on, but the forty-some-odd messages in her inbox worried her. Mail from the office told her the press showed up there as well, but her staff assured her they had it under control.

They also recommended she stay away from the office. The building wasn't "secure."

Tossing the phone on the bed, she paced through the bedroom. The housekeeper told her there were some nightgowns in the dresser and fresh pajamas—all recent purchases, and set aside for guests. Not that she had an overnight bag, or her book, or anything to do...

Abandoning the bedroom, she wandered through the quiet apartment—too quiet. The staff didn't live in. She wasn't sure who mentioned that to her, but they were just a phone call away. Star four on the phone would ring to the valet and he would take care of everything.

Valet.

*THEY RODE in the back of a luxurious limousine, the deep leather seats sumptuous and if not for Charlie's hand wrapped firmly around her own, she might have drowned in the surrealism of it all. The hours since the knock on the door had raced past. His security had shuttled them from their meager apartment, whisking them to the airport in the back of an SUV and through private gates, taking them all the way to a waiting plane.*

*Her heart ached for him, but as the hours passed, Charlie seemed to vanish before her eyes. His jaw tightened, his eyes grew more remote and even his manner became more autocratic, isolated and aloof. Except he still held her hand, held it tightly. Through the window she glimpsed an estate—no, not an estate.*

*A palace.*

*Apprehension shivered across her skin and her pulse raced. What the hell was she doing here? She had finals to take, though she'd been told by a man with a very no-nonsense accent "arrangements would be made."*

*What arrangements?*

*The car glided almost silently past tall iron gates and four heavily armed and decorated military men who stood watch.*

*When they finally pulled up to the circular drive in front of the palace doors, her stomach sank. An entire line of people awaited them—all dressed in black-and-white suits or uniform dresses, save for an older woman with dark hair shot through with strands of silver. She wore a far more ornate black dress, black gloves covered her hands, gems gleamed at her wrists, ears—and dear God, she wore a tiara.*

*A tiara.*

*Anna worried she might throw up. Two younger men accompanied the grand lady and behind her gathered others in equally formal, if stiffly dark, dress. Of course it's dark, Anna chastised herself. They're in mourning. All at once, her attention went back to Charlie. He stared out the window, a muscle ticking in his jaw. The vehicle halted and one of the butlers stepped up to open the door.*

*"I have to exit first," he murmured in a dull voice. Charlie's hand trembled in hers—or maybe*

*she imagined it. He withdrew his touch and pulled away.*

*"Alright," she replied, but he stepped out of the vehicle and the moment his foot touched the ground, everyone along the line bowed or dipped into a curtsy —every single one of them. The band around her chest constricted, threatening to cut off her oxygen. Charlie's chin came up and his hands fell to his sides as he surveyed all of them.*

*He wasn't Charlie anymore. He was everything noble and regal—he'd become the prince.*

*Her Charlie was a prince.*

*After a long pause, Charlie stepped forward and kissed the older woman's cheek. The man holding the car door held out a hand to her and she finally unfolded from the seat to exit the car. In her jeans and T-shirt, she felt positively rumpled next to all of the finery—even the staff wore better outfits than she did.*

*"If you'll follow Elsie, ma'am, she can show you to your room and help you change." The man's crisp words dragged her attention away from Charlie—no, not Charlie.*

*Armand.*

SHE PACED through the darkened living room. The nighttime view was just as spectacular as she'd imagined. The city lights gleamed like a scattering of multicolored gems. She rummaged through the kitchen until she found bottled water tucked into a drawer in the fridge and a container with cake in it—chocolate chocolate cake with chocolate icing. Scoring a fork from another drawer, she made sure everything was back in its place before carrying her stolen treasure into the living room.

The remotes were easily located, hidden beneath a stack of newspapers. Some were written in languages she didn't recognize, but most seemed focused on the business sections. She could imagine Armand sitting here with his morning coffee and reading through each paper as he considered how to dominate the world next.

Her conscience twinged. *In all fairness, he's never talked about ruling the world or wanting anything more than a double cheeseburger with a strawberry shake.* Even the news reports tended to follow two threads with the Grand Duke Andraste—who he was screwing and what charity he supported.

The women in his life—how could she ever have competed with any of them? He dated the crème de la crème of the world's most beautiful women.

Setting aside the newspapers, she grabbed the remote and pointed it at the screen. It shouldn't have surprised her that the channel was already on the gossip station, but she comforted the disappointment with a bite of cake.

"The big news this morning was whether one of the world's most eligible bachelors, ranked number seven by both *Sophisticate* and *Scantily* magazines, is indeed off the market." An image zoomed in of her getting into the SUV outside her house. The sadness etched into her expression

HEATHER LONG

filled the screen. Despite the sunglasses, her mouth was a soft, thin line and her face was pale. The wind stirred her hair and pulled one strand across—she barely remembered that part.

She remembered looking at the crowd and all the camera lenses zooming back at her.

"Anna Novak, a Los Angeles businesswoman who was recently appointed the head of the Princess Alyxandretta Dagmar Scholarship Fund for Foster Children—"

She grimaced at the name. That was not what the scholarship would be called, but the reporter's phrasing seemed to diminish the project —as if it weren't important.

"—is working closely with the prince as he brings the fund under the oversight of the Dagmar Foundation. The foundation as we have reported is Grand Duke Armand's pet project and has been since he founded it nearly a decade ago."

Licking the frosting off the fork slowly, Anna paused. She hadn't realized he began the foundation himself.

"Like many royals, the grand duke travels frequently and spends a great deal of money furthering the causes closest to his heart. His long-established bachelorhood has never been in this much question before. ACE has learned that Anna Novak and the prince attended college together and according to Vance Anderson, the couple lived together..."

The screen changed and a man with a weak jaw and a hint of jowls smiled at the camera. "We were in economics together, I think it was their first class in freshman year—could be wrong. Anyway, they dated a lot and were pretty inseparable. I noticed because she was hot and they moved in together just a couple of months later—"

"It was a year later, jackass." Anna stabbed the cake again and gave herself another chocolategasm to numb the stupidity of that interview. She didn't recognize the name and the man looked vaguely familiar, but that could just be his build and conversation.

"In the meanwhile, the prince's former flame, the model Nikole, had this to say..." The reporter blathered on.

The screen cut away to a close-up with the gorgeous Somalian beauty with the caramel-dipped-in-gold skin and too-blue eyes. "Hmm, I do not believe there is much to this relationship beyond the press speculation. As lovely as a happily ever after would be, if she were that important, he would have mentioned her to me, *n'est-ce pas?*"

Anna scowled and stuffed another bite of cake in her mouth. The woman continued to talk about her most recent vacation with the prince—less than a month before—and the only reason they weren't together at the moment was her photo shoot in Greece.

Licking the chocolate off her lip, Anna punched the fork into the cake again. If only it were that snotty, arrogant woman's face. The irrational anger at the other woman wasn't remotely Nikole's fault. Didn't make it go away though. Blowing out a breath, she was glad when the reporter switched tracks and an image of Alyx filled the screen.

"It was just a few months ago that the grand duke was reunited with his cousin, Grand Duchess Alyxandretta, who unbeknownst to the family grew up in foster care in California. Sources close to the family have stated categorically that had the family known of the princess's existence, they would have reunited with her sooner and are profoundly grateful to have the opportunity to welcome the darling princess and her new husband." The camera angle switched and the blonde reporter turned to look at the camera. "The prince and his brothers attended the small wedding ceremony in Sacramento and the grand reception later. The princess will be presented to the European contingent and allies this coming New Year's at a special ball in her honor. But the question on everyone's lips is will the grand duke be escorting Anna Novak and do the ladies of the world have to give up on their chances of dreaming this prince will come for them?"

She rolled her eyes. Could they become any more melodramatic?

"To add to the mystery spice of this secret love affair, ACE has learned that in the decade since their split, Anna Novak has been engaged twice—"

She choked.

"—her first engagement took place just two

years following the reported breakup with the then recently ascended Andraste Grand Duke, Armand Dagmar. As you may recall, the grand duke's father and titular head of the family passed away from a heart attack during the prince's senior year at college. Sources have reported that when the prince returned to the family estate in Norway, Anna Novak actually accompanied him but left before the final ceremony that sealed the grand duke's new role. Two years after this, announcements were posted in the Tampa, Florida, newspaper regarding her engagement to firefighter Chad Dowds. ACE requested an interview with Mister Dowds this afternoon, but he refused to answer our questions."

*Oh crap.* She needed to call Chad and apologize.

"Her second engagement, however, is the one that interested local reporter April Menendez—" The screen cut away to a lovely Hispanic woman standing in front of a Los Angeles police station.

"Thank you, Kim. I'm standing here at police station in Los Angeles where a certain detective works. Four years ago, this police detective—who has not allowed us to use his name—was engaged to Anna Novak. Because the officer works undercover, ACE was allowed to interview him but only if we did not take cameras inside or use his image. The officer in question had nothing but praise for Miss Novak. He wouldn't comment on their engagement or why it ended. He also dismissed the prince's involvement in calling off his engagement to Miss Novak, assuring us that it was a mutual decision."

"April." The screen cut back to the woman in the studio—she angled so it appeared she was speaking right to the image of April in the upper right hand of the screen. "Have you had a chance to sit down with Miss Novak?"

"No, Kim. I haven't. All attempts to reach Miss Novak have been rebuffed, though we have it on good authority that she was seen entering the prince's Petersburg Towers here in Los Angeles. Now, as we reported last month, the prince maintains a residence at the top of the tower. His security also picked her up at her house." The image cut to the circus outside her little cottage and Anna sighed. "As of ten this evening, Miss Novak had not returned home. Her office is declining any comment as has the spokesman for the royal family..."

Richard was shown leaving an office somewhere in Los Angeles. He nodded politely to the cameras, but kept right on walking.

"...so at this time, it's anyone's gamble. But I have to say that if the two have reunited, then it has all the fairytale potential a woman could dream of..."

"Thanks, April." The screen focused back to the studio. "For those just joining us, we are following the breaking story of Prince Armand's love affair with American Anna Novak. Are they a match made in storybook heaven or will she break his heart for a second time?"

*Break his heart...* Anna stared at the screen as

it cut to a commercial advertising nude celebrity moments. She looked at the remains of her decimated cake. The trip to Norway was one of the hardest she'd ever taken—but it was nothing compared to the flight home.

Alone.

"You shouldn't watch that. You'll never hear anything you want to hear." Armand's quiet voice wrapped around her. She found him standing a few feet behind her, his hands in his pockets, exhaustion digging grooves deep into the furrows around his eyes.

"You're back." And she had no idea how she felt about it.

"My apologies. I didn't expect to take as long as I did." He walked around to sit down on the sofa next to her—fall down was more like it. He claimed the remote and hit the mute button when the reporter started talking again. "You found the cake?"

"Yeah. It's good." Discomfort shifted inside her. He looked like hell. "Should you be going out with those threats?"

He slid off his shoes and stretched his legs out until his feet rested on the coffee table. "I cannot allow others to dictate where I can and cannot go. If that were the case, I would never leave home."

She maneuvered the cake around in the container, chewing her lower lip. "But it's not safe—"

"Anna, it's never been safe. The unhappy accident of my DNA means I live with security twenty-four hours a day, seven days a week. We take precautions, I let them do their job and they allow me to live my life."

What a horrible life that must have been... "How did you manage to go to school? You weren't surrounded by security."

He leaned over and poked a finger into the bowl, scraping some chocolate from the rim. "Wasn't I?"

"I think I would have noticed." Security didn't exactly blend into the background.

Armand swiped another finger full of the frosting and she scooped some onto a fork and held it out to him. He stared at her for a long heartbeat and then accepted the bite. A streak of chocolate decorated his lower lip. She stared at it until his tongue swiped it away. "Jimmy Snozen from across the hall."

"What?"

"Jimmy Snozen. Giles Carter. Mike Denning. Eddie Brown." He ticked the four names off on his fingers.

"They were your frat brothers." *They hung out at the apartment and they moved in next door and across the hall when we did...*

He shook his head slowly. "No. They were part of the security detail, as was the pizza delivery man, the Chinese takeout and the sandwich shop guy." He grabbed her water bottle from the cushion where it rested next to her leg and unscrewed the top. "May I?"

"Sure."

A long drink later, he put the cap back onto it.

"Why?" The one question she never asked. The one she always worried about the answer. "Why...why were they dressed like that? Why did they act like your friends? Is—was Rick?"

"No. Richard and I met just like I said we did. He was my assigned roommate freshman year. Security vetted him, but he came up clean, so they let it happen. As for why—because I wanted to go to school without men in suits keeping everyone at arm's length. I wanted to be me and not the royal representative of the family." He leaned his head back. He caught her legs and swung her feet up until they rested in his lap. It was so heart-achingly familiar a gesture, she didn't think to pull away.

The screen flickered through another set of images, more photos of him and so many other women. She looked back at the real thing.

"I know you hate me right now and with good reason." Her heart squeezed at the empty acceptance in those words. "I know the last place you want to be is here. I messed this up and for that, I am truly, deeply sorry. But will you stay? Stay with me until I can fix this and you can be safe?" The quiet question carried such a deep longing that she couldn't find irritation with it, even if she didn't want to answer it.

She stretched out to set the container and its fork on the coffee table. "I'll stay. For as long as it takes."

When he didn't say anything, she glanced over and found his eyes closed, his breathing regular.

He'd fallen asleep.

Stretching carefully, she reached over to the other chair and snagged a throw blanket. She spread it over them both, because he still held her legs captive. She found a way to be comfortable and switched the station to a black-and-white movie. She watched him, not the movie, until her eyelids grew too heavy.

*Did I break your heart?*

Did she dare ask?

# CHAPTER 6
# ARMAND

He hadn't expected to fall asleep and he'd even less expected her to stay there. But the crick in his neck and the cramp in his back were well worth the trouble —especially when he found her sound asleep next to him, her bare feet still resting in his lap and beneath his hands. If only the peace of that moment extended to three hours later in the meeting with his head of security.

"We've gone over this, Anna. Peterson can't secure your office—not in its current location." He glanced at his security chief. The man nodded, his solemn expression adding gravity to the statement.

"His Highness is correct, Miss Novak. It would take us a week to complete the threat assessment properly, install a new system and bulletproof glass. The parking structure is not secure, so we would have to invest in more security for your vehicle—though we could handle transport ourselves. Either way, the threat ratio is not in your favor." The man laid it out, cleanly and without bias.

The disappointment on Anna's face, however, tugged at Armand's heart. "However—and this is just a suggestion." Arresting his need—and habit—to take over took some forethought. He'd considered the options all morning, when he wasn't staring at her eating or drinking or just breathing. "The fourteenth floor is available."

"I'm sorry, what?" She pulled her attention back to the meeting and focused on him. The weariness in her expression smoothed, the invisible barrier, the curtain that seemed to have dropped between them for so brief a time the night before, firmly in place again.

"The fourteenth floor." He repeated and tapped two fingers against the tabletop. "It's unoccupied and has about three thousand square feet of office space available and another thousand square feet for a security office. The building is secure, it won't take us long to arrange for the entire office to be moved here."

Resistance flared in her gaze, but she merely nodded. "That is a generous offer, Armand." She moistened her lips. "But it's a great deal of trouble to go to—particularly to pay for such a large space."

He smiled at the use of his name. It didn't carry the same affection as Charlie or the same depth of meaning, but it was far preferable to "Your Highness."

"It really is no trouble at all. We own the

building and I would be delighted to donate the floor to the cause."

"A floor in this tower would serve better, Miss Novak." Peterson didn't require any encouragement to pile on. "The building is secure, the garage is secure and we have a full-time rotating staff, which means your on-duty detail wouldn't be stretched—"

"My on-duty what?" She whipped her gaze over to pin the security chief. "I have a detail? Isn't that...going too far?"

"No, ma'am. A standard detail of five will be assigned to you, led by Johnson." He nodded to the tall man who arranged to have her picked up at her house.

Anna rubbed her forehead and dropped her gaze to the table. "Would you all excuse us, please?"

Peterson glanced at him for permission. Armand nodded and the men filed out. He forced himself to lean back in the chair rather than reach across and touch her hand. "You okay?"

"No." She looked up and a smile strained the lines around her mouth. "No, I'm not."

He sat forward and reached a hand across to her. She stared at it and then him before sliding her cold fingers against his palm. "You're freezing." Squeezing her hand, he rose, releasing her only long enough to walk around and strip off his suit coat. He claimed the chair next to her and draped the coat around her shoulders. Capturing her hands again, he rubbed them lightly.

"Do you live like this? All the time? Security details? Threat assessments?"

He shrugged. Telling her a lie might ease the worry and tension from her face, but... "You get used to it. There have always been threats against my family. At one time, there was even a bounty on my grandfather's head. The communist regime at the time wanted to stifle any more tales of the family's return to Mother Russia."

"Yeah, that's not comforting." But she smiled and the soft curve to her lips beckoned him. It took everything in him to walk away the day before, but as much as he'd already botched their reunion, he refused to let anger spoil it.

"It wasn't meant to be comforting—it's hard to let others take over these areas—but it's essential for your safety." Her fingers continued to tremble in his grip. It was damn hard not to just pull her close. "What can I do to make this easier for you?"

Her mouth twisted, but the smile didn't fade. "Well, you're not making fun of me—that's a good start."

"When have I ever made fun of you?" Askance, he raised both eyebrows.

"When I wanted to backpack across Europe. When I took that theory class from Doctor Ramuesen...oh and when I picked up that wardrobe at the garage sale. You laughed at me for four hours." Her nose wrinkled, but the strain around her eyes eased.

He burst out laughing. "You hated walking across campus and you planned to sling on a pack and walk across Europe? Not to mention, have you ever stayed in a hostel? The smell is pretty bad."

"Fine. Maybe I wouldn't have done as well with Europe." She snorted a noise that sounded suspiciously like a laugh.

"And Dr. Ramuesen was a whackjob with a pen. His idea of diplomacy was to close borders based on language—only those with similar languages were bound to understand the other side, translators be damned." He still chuckled but shook his head. "The man wouldn't know diplomacy if it bit him in the ass. He was turned down by the U.S. State Department four times and if I recall, you were furious at his grade for your midterm paper."

"Because he gave me a C when I pointed out the flaws in the Treaty of Versailles based on his law of language." Outrage sparkled amid the laughter in her eyes and her hand tightened on his.

"Wholly undeserved." He soothed. "Though, you finished the class even if you disliked him."

"Yeah." She bit her lip. "I still have the wardrobe."

"That ugly behemoth?" He couldn't bottle the words before they popped out. She tipped her head at him and gave him a sly smile.

"It wasn't ugly. It had—has character."

Doubtful, he stared at her.

"Okay, fine. It's ugly as sin, and it weighs five tons, but I like it." She made a face and he laughed, allowing himself the barest of touches down her cheek with the backs of his fingers.

"You love it and that's why I didn't argue when you insisted on moving it into the bedroom..."

"Oh God." Her eyes rounded, then she grimaced.

"What?" A quick glance around the room showed they were still alone.

"I made your security guys carry it up the stairs."

He laughed again. "They didn't mind."

"Of course they did—they complained about how heavy it was and I gave away your fancy European lager to pay for it."

It was his turn to grimace. "*That* I know. I came home from class to find it all gone and Eddie toasted me with his that night."

She giggled, a delicious, girly, youthful titter, and the rock on his chest rolled to the side. "This is weird." She withdrew her hands and he hated it, but he let her go. She wasn't so pale or so cold, warmth flushed her cheeks.

"I don't know—it feels pretty normal to me." Seductively normal—they used to have conversations like this all the time. "Are you hungry? I'm hungry." He rose and held a hand out to her. She'd barely eaten breakfast.

They could definitely use the distraction before he picked her up to cuddle away the fears. Patience, however, was not the virtue he wanted to embrace at the moment. She stared at his hand for a heartbeat longer than made him happy, but she took it and he tugged her to her feet. Interlacing his fingers with hers, he led the way toward the kitchen, but she pulled back and he halted.

"What?"

"We should give them an answer so they don't stand out there in the hall waiting for us to call them back in." She turned toward the door and he went with her rather than letting her pull away. She opened the door and peeked out.

"Your Highness, Miss Novak." Peterson glanced up from his phone.

"Mr. Peterson, if we're going to be working together, would you mind just calling me Anna?" She didn't like titles—amusing considering how often she threw his in his face. But he squelched the thought.

"Of course, Miss Anna. Have you reached a decision?" Peterson didn't miss a beat, the man accepted the invitation and took them right back to business. It was why Armand put him in charge of his U.S. security forces. He was damn good at his job after nearly two decades in law enforcement and a stint with the FBI.

"Yes. The fourteenth floor would be lovely—if it will be less trouble for all of you." She smiled and it lit her whole face up. Armand squashed the first lick of jealousy that his security chief earned that expression before he did.

"Absolutely. We'll take care of it. It will only take a couple of days. We'll start with background checks on the staff so we can get them in immediately—"

"Would you mind if we went down to see the space?" Anna didn't look at him, but when Peterson did, her jaw tightened.

Nodding his assent, Armand followed all of them into the hall and to the elevator.

Peterson touched a finger to his ear. "Lock down the fourteenth."

Anna folded her arms but made no attempt to remove his jacket. Sliding his hands into his pockets, Armand watched her silent, stiff frame for the duration of the elevator ride. The doors opened to the freshly refurbished floor. He had to touch her arm to keep her from exiting before Johnson and Peterson. Her lips thinned and he dropped the contact with a sweeping motion to allow her to precede him.

Carefully decorated in creams and earth tones, the floor resembled the one he maintained an office on. The space was vast and open. "It's huge," Anna murmured, turning in a slow circle as though to absorb it all.

"Yes, ma'am." Peterson paced her with Johnson remaining at the elevator. "We can have temporary walls erected and modified to your specifications. It won't take more than a day or so."

"I have meetings this afternoon and tomorrow morning."

Armand kept his own counsel until she spoke. "You can cancel those."

"Actually—" she pivoted and faced him, "—I can't. One is with Derrick Milton, he's one of the prime candidates for the scholarship and flagged as a high risk to stay in school. He needs the meeting as much as I do."

"What kind of a risk?" Peterson inserted his question before Armand could ask the same.

Anna scowled. "Not a physical threat. Academic risk. He's in his fourth foster home of the year, he's been acting out and he turns eighteen in three weeks. We classify that as a high risk to even stay in school. At eighteen, he'll be legally free to walk away from his foster home, drop school and vanish and no one can do anything about it. He's got great grades, though, and loads of potential. I will *not* risk him further by canceling a meeting I had to tie myself into a knot to get him to agree to in the first place."

Flush with color, she lit up from the inside out with her passion and temper kindled in her eyes. "Give Peterson the address and details."

She blinked rapidly. "Really?"

Did his agreement surprise her so much? Burying the fresh slice her lack of faith cut in him, he nodded. "Of course. You have your life and it's for the foundation."

Anna pulled out her phone and forwarded an email with the details to Peterson. His security chief glanced down at his phone. "If you'll excuse me, Your Highness, Miss Novak. I'll make arrangements. Johnson will remain."

"I'll need to pick up someone from my office, though. To take notes—"

"We have a woman on staff we can loan you for the time being—Kate Braddock. Her checks are already completed so she can fill in the gaps."

Peterson named one of her female security guards, a detail he'd discussed with Armand the night before. Anna might resist close-quarters monitoring, but they could put someone on her immediate staff and Miss Braddock's credentials were impeccable.

"Oh, this is very sensitive work—" Anna hedged, her teeth pulling at her lower lip.

"Why don't you meet Miss Braddock?" Armand tired of her looking to Peterson. He wanted her attention on him. She didn't respond well to orders, but perhaps he could coax her. "It couldn't hurt to meet her, yes? And if she's suitable, it will help to keep your schedule from being disrupted any more than necessary."

She wavered, pressing a hand to her mouth and glancing around the empty space again. Dwarfed by his jacket, she looked indescribably vulnerable. "You're right." Two words he never thought he'd hear her say. "It can't hurt to meet her. Is it possible to do it now?"

"Of course." Peterson paced away from them and pressed a button on his earpiece, his voice fading as he walked toward the elevator. "Please send Miss Braddock to the fourteenth floor..."

Alone, Armand prowled after Anna as she began to walk through the space to the window. "Thank you."

"Shouldn't that be my line?" The snap in her response didn't diminish the fact that she spoke to him again.

"You're accepting a lot of very abrupt changes

with grace." Would she allow him to pay her compliment or not? "I appreciate it."

"Well, it's not about me, is it?" She put two fingers on the glass and looked down at the street. "It's about the people the scholarship can help."

He disagreed but kept it to himself. "Why is it so important to you?"

Impatience creased her expression and she gave him a reproachful look. "I'm a scholarship kid, Cha—Your Highness."

"Armand." Reminding her would become a habit if she kept trying to put the barriers back up between them.

"I don't know *Armand*." She traced a pattern on the window with her fingernail. "And I'm a scholarship kid. Every penny of my education came from scholarships like this one, and from the jobs I took. Not everyone is born with a silver spoon."

Irritated at the slam, he leaned against the glass and studied her profile. "I know. You should be proud of what you accomplished. I just wanted to know why these kids were so important to you."

"Because they aren't important to anyone else." She chewed on her lower lip and all he wanted to do was lick along the soft skin to nurse the hurt. "They get forgotten, shuttled to the side, put off over and over again. No one makes them first on their list. I had to jump through hoops to get this kid to agree to the meeting. He doesn't think there's a point, so I have to prove to him there is. *Everyone* deserves a chance to fly."

"I hate that Alyx grew up that way," he admitted. It lacerated his soul to think of anyone in his family feeling unwanted.

"I really like her." Anna met his gaze and smiled a little. "She's funny. But her funny covers up a lot of pain."

"I know, her husband is very good for her, though. He makes her truly smile." Daniel Voldakov would not have been anyone's first choice to marry into the family—his Bolshevik roots, his American mannerisms, even his fervent disregard for protocol. But none of it mattered. Not when he adored the princess.

*And without him, we wouldn't have found Alyx.*

"He's an interesting man." Admiration crept into her voice and ignited his anger all over again. "He's *married*."

The softness in her expression turned tense. "I'm aware of that, I just said he's interesting. I've only met him once when I was having lunch with Alyx. Don't play the jealous lover, Your Highness. It doesn't suit you."

The elevator dinged and Anna jerked back a step. Her cheeks went rosy again. She'd forgotten about Kyle—a fact made clear by her faltering look at the security guard and her unsteady smile at the blonde making her way toward them.

Aggravated with his own lack of control, Armand bit back the urge to order the other woman to wait so he and Anna could finish their discussion. "I'll leave you to meet with Miss Braddock."

Striding away before he could change his mind, he refused to glance behind and see if she felt his absence as keenly as he experienced hers. In the elevator, he shook his head. He wasn't a college student anymore—and had no business behaving like some overeager boy on his first date. Glancing up at the camera, he considered his next steps. "I want reports of her afternoon and alert Peterson I'm going out."

Withdrawing his phone from his pocket, he dialed Richard's number. A grueling game of racquetball might take the edge off and give him time to clear his head.

~

## ANNA

Kate Braddock turned out to be brilliant. "All right, I've contacted your office and downloaded the application materials and his latest grade reports as well as the essay his English teacher submitted."

The first round of scholarships would go to teens identified and nominated from the local school districts. Thirty candidates had made the final cut and it was up to Anna to identify the first ten. She really wanted Derrick to be one of those ten. "Can you scan the essay? I remember reading a quote from *Great Expectations*." After spending five minutes with the other woman, she'd taken solace in the idea that Kate understood exactly what she'd need.

Armand had disappeared again, and when she'd asked Johnson, he'd only replied that the grand duke wasn't available. Irritated, she focused on the meeting in front of her rather than the SUV she rode in or the two cars traveling one in front and one in back. As much as she resented the interference, the photograph of her sleeping in her bed popped into her mind and she had to fight away a fresh shiver of fear.

"I have it..." Kate glanced up.

"Go ahead." Work. She needed to work, to think about Derrick, about how to persuade him to take charge of his own future.

"'Whatever I acquired, I tried to impart to Joe. This statement sounds so well that I can't in my conscience let it pass unexplained. I wanted to make Joe less ignorant and common, that he might be worthier of my society and less open to Estella's reproach.'" Kate stroked her finger across the screen to turn the page of the young man's essay. It had captured Anna's attention from the first time she'd read through his work. The rest of the team had felt the same way.

Kate continued. "This resonates because Pip is so caught up in the appearances of things that he feels like gentlemanly behavior can be caught, like a cold. While a person cannot be more than who they are, it is true that exposure to culture can have an ameliorating effect on a person's behavior, choices, and goal setting. I appreciate Pip's value of knowledge, particularly in the admiration he shows to Miss Havisham and Estella. Unfortunately, it's clear that Pip values the academic pursuits of these two women over the real-world knowledge Joe possesses. It's all well and good to admire what the 'haves' have, but it's better to be aware of how the world really works."

"Haves versus have nots. He admires the concept of a higher education, but doesn't put any practical value in it." Thinking out loud helped Anna organize.

"Or he's simply afraid to believe in a dream." Kate suggested. "Because he does admire it so much, he doesn't put himself in the same class as Miss Havisham or Estella. Like Pip, he doesn't think he'll ever belong so what's the point of dreaming about it?"

"Oh, I think I love you." Anna grinned. "That's it exactly. Okay, I know what to say to him."

"You're welcome." Kate chuckled and checked her watch. "Do you want me in on the meeting with him?"

"I think so, but if I give you a signal do you think you can get everyone to back off a little? I don't want to intimidate him." The last she said with a glance at Kyle.

"Miss Braddock can step out as necessary." Kyle twisted in his seat. "But I will have to insist on staying in the room, Miss Novak."

"Kyle, it's very important that Derrick doesn't feel like we're pressuring him." She wouldn't allow him to be intimidated, not even for her "safety."

"I won't say a word," he promised, but the

man wasn't exactly subtle. Leaning back in the seat, she glanced out the window. They were in North Hollywood and the streets grew more and more residential. Anna had called ahead to let Mrs. Brown, Derrick's foster mother, know they were on their way. She'd sounded so relieved, and Anna had to wonder why.

When they pulled up at the front of the house, she didn't wonder anymore. The lawn boasted a dozen reporters, and nearly twice that many cameras. *Crap.*

"Stay in the car, please, Miss Novak." Kyle touched a hand to his earpiece. "David, head up and make sure Miss Novak's appointment is present in the house." A man exited the lead car and started across the lawn. Two more men stepped out of the car behind them and took up positions on the sidewalk, effectively blocking the press from coming anywhere near the car.

Kate touched her hand and Anna realized— belatedly—she'd clenched her fists. "We'll take care of it. Worst-case scenario, we'll make arrangements to bring Derrick with us and take the meeting somewhere else."

On the porch, a young dark-skinned man answered the door and the cameras seemed to divide their attention between the cars and him. His eyes widened and he backed up, but David had already turned to intercept one of the reporters.

"All right, Miss Novak, what do you want to do?" Kyle glanced at her. Tension knotted in Anna's belly, hard and fierce.

"I want to talk to Derrick." And apologize. *Good God, that poor kid.* Hot on the heels of her anxiety came anger. How dare the press subject a kid to this? He had nothing to do with Armand or the ridiculous gossip piece.

"Clear the lawn," Kyle ordered into his ear-piece and then picked up his cell phone and punched in a number. "This is Kyle Johnson," he began and rattled off the address. "We have several members of the press trespassing and causing a hazard on the street..." He paused. "Thank you."

"Miss Novak, you stay in the car until I open the door, we go in the same way we exited your house yesterday. I want you right at my back."

"What about Kate?" The poor woman certainly didn't need to be jammed into this.

"I'll be right behind." Kate gave her hand a squeeze. "And I'll have your bag."

Anna nodded, still not entirely certain of all of this. It took some hustling, but Kyle got her up the walk and onto the porch just as a police car arrived. Kate and Kyle followed Anna inside when Derrick admitted them, but the others stayed out.

"Derrick." Anna extended her hand. "I'm Anna Novak, we've spoken on the phone."

Uneasy, the kid still took her hand and shook it briefly. "Sorry about the zoo, Miss Novak."

"It's hardly your fault." She followed Derrick to the kitchen. Though the house was definitely older and showing signs of wear, it was clean and neatly kept.

"It's Mrs. Brown's fault." Derrick scowled.

"She saw a news report about you this morning and when you called to confirm, she called them."

"Oh. Well...I'm still sorry that they're out there, but I didn't come to talk about the press. I came to talk about your future. Do you think we can sit down and chat for a bit?"

He shifted, eyeing Kate and then Kyle, before bringing his attention back to her. "Ma'am, if you don't mind my saying—people like you and I— we don't generally mix."

Pulling out a chair from the tiny oaken breakfast set, Anna sat down and looked at the one opposite her. Derrick hesitated but took a perch. Crossing one leg over the other, she took a deep breath. Every word from this moment forward had to count. "When I was your age, I had two choices. Go to the local community college my parents could afford if I worked part-time or apply to several scholarship funds and go to the four-year school I'd been accepted at..."

# CHAPTER 7
# ARMAND

I t was late afternoon by the time he returned to the tower. Anna was still out—or so Peterson reported to him on the elevator ride up. Unfortunately, a dozen reporters at the North Hollywood house had greeted Anna. Pride filled him, despite the interference of the press she'd held up beautifully. Her security team performed as expected and reported in regularly.

They had no new leads on who leaked her name to the press. Peterson did have a theory, though, and it was one Armand did not care for. His head of security speculated that Armand's lingering presence in California had led to local reporters researching previous connections that might be present. Chances were, they'd looked into his past years at college and Anna's proximity had given them a clue.

Their meeting served only as the final trigger. Showering off the sweat, he'd changed and walked back into the living room in time to see the front door open. Anna walked in, still wearing his suit coat from earlier. For the barest moment, he had a glimpse of the weariness in her eyes.

"I'll let His Highness know when everything is ready," Kyle told her and then his gaze flicked past her to meet Armand's. He inclined his head. "Your Highness."

"Thank you, Johnson." The man headed for the elevator and Armand shut the door and locked it. Anna set her bags down stiffly.

"Have you eaten?"

She shook her head. "We didn't exactly have the time."

Eyeing her, he reached out and took her hand and tugged her toward the kitchen. She was quiet —too quiet—and he let her hand go and opened the refrigerator. "What's wrong now?"

"Nothing." Her flattened tone gave her away.

He cut a glance toward her from the corner of his eye. "Uh-huh. I know that nothing. What's wrong?"

"Nothing is wrong." She padded around to the breadbox and pulled out a loaf. His coat dwarfed her, but rather than tug it off, she'd slid her arms into the sleeves and hugged it to her like a robe.

"Hmm, it doesn't sound like nothing." She chose bread, so he opened the drawers till he found lunchmeats and cheeses. "In fact, it sounds a lot like something."

"No. It sounds like nothing. Because that's all it is, nothing." She opened and shut the cabinets until she found plates. He added mayonnaise, mustard and pickle relish—something he enjoyed—to the gathering of sandwich fixings on the counter.

"But you said it with a tone." A tone he remembered all too well—a tone that said nothing meant everything and ignoring it would just cause a fight.

The last thing he wanted.

She circled the island and made it to the pantry ahead of him. She pulled out three bags. One each of pretzels, chips and dried apple crisps. They circled each other, dodging with an expert ease. Anna added the bags to the counter, setting each item at an exact angle and in the order they'd need to build sandwiches.

"I didn't say it with a *tone*." Her voice climbed a half note with exasperation.

"You did." He pulled open a drawer and took out a knife. He flipped the bread onto the plates and nudged the drawer shut with his hip. "Your shoulders are stiff, your eyes are tired and there's tension in your jaw. You were uneasy earlier but willing to work with us. This afternoon, you're tense, solemn and quiet—ergo, your nothing is definitely something."

"Oh for the love of God, Charlie. Let it go." She banged her hands against the island for emphasis.

He cocked his head to the side and met her irritation steadily. "No. This only works if we talk —not if we ignore it."

"What this? Making sandwiches requires conversation?"

Counting to twenty in his head—in three languages—helped. "Being together. We left a lot unsaid—and I'd rather we didn't add any more items to that list. You're going to be staying here and we're going to spend a lot of time together." He ignored the internal fist pump at the idea—it lacked a certain decorum and he was pretty certain she wouldn't appreciate the gesture.

He spread mayonnaise onto the bread, added a layer of mustard across it and chose three slices of Swiss and two of the turkey before repeating the process with the top slice of bread.

"We're working together. There's a difference." The deflection was so poor it didn't deserve a comment.

"We have a personal history that cannot be filed and put away." He stacked the sandwich together and cut it in half before sliding the plate over to her. Flipping his own bread over, he added the relish and a very thin smear of mustard to opposite pieces of bread. He added turkey, ham and American cheese to his. Sparing her a glance, he found her staring at her sandwich. "Now what's wrong?"

"You—you—" She stuttered. She never stuttered. It was almost as endearing as the fact that she called him Charlie.

"You still like your water in a bottle, your turkey with lots of Swiss and you hate mustard with any other type of sandwich. Now eat it— you're too pale." He released her gaze and finished fixing his, taking the time to put the lids back on the containers. But rather than eat, she put it all away and he sighed.

"This is hard——" She spoke to the refrigerator, but he would take what he could get. She put the items back in slowly, too slowly.

"I know. I wish I could make it easier for you."

"No——believe it or not, the whole death threat thing, that's still surreal and not really sinking in. Being here with you——that's what's hard." She rearranged the condiment shelf, putting like with like.

Adding order to chaos.

"I don't know what to call you. Is your name Armand or is it Charlie? Should I say Your Highness—which apparently you don't like—or maybe Mister Dagmar? Or is it Andraste...? I don't know how to do this..." She turned, closing the fridge. Her expression was tense and stricken. "The press was all over that boy's house and he handled it beautifully. I have a dozen more kids just like him that I have to meet. How do I do that with the press on my heels? What am I supposed to do?"

"You can eat your sandwich." He set down his and wiped his hands on a napkin before reaching over to open her water bottle and setting it next to her plate. "Then you can drink your water. Unless you prefer coffee... I don't have soda, but I can certainly order some."

He picked up his sandwich and took a bite.

"That's it? Just eat my sandwich?" The dangerous tone was back in her voice. The same one she used when she replied *nothing* earlier.

"For now. You need to eat. You've had a lot of shocks to your system——" Mustard splattered him. He blinked and looked down at the remains of the half sandwich that struck his face and dripped down onto his shirt.

She smiled at him and took a bite out of the half she hadn't thrown at him.

Plucking the bread and cheese and turkey took a moment, he set them down calmly on the edge of his plate before he hit the base of the chip bag. The compressed air burst the end and showered her in potato chips.

Her eyes went wide and he smiled.

They both lunged for the water bottle, but between them, it fired the water up and showered it down on both of them. Anna had chips in her hair. Mustard clung to his chin. They both dripped. Their gazes collided and she laughed—a deep, belly-rolling laugh that smashed the tension against the rocks—and he grinned...before hitting her with another douse of water from the unused bottle.

# CHAPTER 8
## ANNA

A hysterical fit of the giggles assaulted her when the water splashed against her face. Chilled from the fridge, it soaked right through her silk shirt and sent a wave of goose bumps racing over her skin—but she wasn't cold. Not like she felt when she'd arrived back at his penthouse. Heat warmed her face and her cheeks ached from holding back her smile—Charlie chased her around the island until he'd dumped the entire contents of the bottle over her head.

She scampered, grabbing a bottle of ketchup from the fridge on her slide by. Whirling, she flipped the cap off and pointed it at him.

"You wouldn't dare." But his eyes challenged her and his grin was as feral as it was excited. She squeezed the bottle and he dodged—the ketchup shot across the kitchen in a stream and splatted against the chest of a very nicely dressed, younger version of Armand.

"Oh crap." She winced.

The man stared at her drolly as ketchup dripped down the expensive fabric to splat against the floor. Armand glanced from her to the newcomer and straightened. He stepped right in front of her, cutting off her view. "George." He pronounced it *Shorge* and his accent sharpened. "You weren't expected."

His brother.

*Fantastic.*

The last time she'd seen the younger prince, he'd been barely sixteen, scrawny and long limbed. Heart sinking, she closed the lid on the ketchup.

"Clearly, and I wasn't aware you were entertaining." Disdain rolled through the too-cool tone. "But Peterson informed me that all family needed to check in."

Armand glanced over his shoulder at her and his gaze flicked from her face to her chest and back up again. She lifted her eyebrows and looked down. Embarrassment surged and she pulled his damp jacket closed. The water soaked right through the silk shirt, clearly outlining her breasts, and her nipples stood out in stark relief.

George walked over to tug a paper towel from the dispenser and blotted at the ketchup.

"I'm sorry about that," she began, looking for the right words to dress the apology up in...

*I'm sorry you walked in and I sprayed you with ketchup? I'll pay for your suit cleaning? Don't mind the wet T-shirt contest.*

Armand's dress shirt clung to him, hugging the smooth, cut lines of his musculature.

He still worked out. They'd run in college—he a lot more than she—but he'd also enjoyed going to the gym. A habit he'd dragged her into—mostly because watching him lift weights was sexy as hell. She cleared her throat. "I should...let you two talk."

"That would be pleasant." Dismissal hung right off the end of George's statement. Armand's back stiffened.

"That was rude." Armand's voice went flat, cool, and she knew that tone—just like his accent —which echoed so loudly in the words. The tone cried angry.

"My apologies, Your Highness. I am unaccustomed to the polite rules that include ruining a five-thousand-dollar suit. It must be an American thing." His brother's tone was equally cold.

She moved out from behind Armand and met the cool disdain in the younger prince's gaze. He barely spared her a glance, as if she weren't worthy of his attention. The silence in the room stretched, and Armand's left hand curled into a fist—the lines around his mouth turned white.

"Of course. It's a completely bourgeois middle-American way of saying suck on it." She beamed and brushed her fingers against Armand's fist. She'd only ever seen him get into two fights before—the first when a guy in a bar dumped his beer all over her. It had been an accident, but the belligerent drunk leered and Armand slugged him. His friends waded right into the brawl that broke out.

Friends—friends who were his security force.

The second had begun as a playful tussle during a flag football match on the field. It escalated so quickly when the other team hit him—and he responded in kind.

But it would be better to not start another brawl in the kitchen. Particularly with him wearing her mustard, mayo and turkey sandwich and both of them soaked from the water play. In fact, the kitchen was quite the disaster.

"Apologize, George." Armand didn't bend, his gaze fixed on his brother. "Now."

The younger prince scowled, but the expression rippled away and disappeared behind a placid, cold remoteness. He turned to look at her and inclined his head in a sharp nod. "My apologies, Miss Novak."

The words were correct, but the tone told her to go to hell. She appreciated the distinction. "Please accept mine as well." Hers lacked the force to penetrate his chilly reception, but in this case—escape might be the better part of valor. "If you gentlemen will excuse me, I'm just going to change and get to work."

Armand's fingers locked around hers and tugged her back. *Or maybe not...*

"George can excuse us. There's a suite downstairs waiting for him." His grip was like silken steel, gentle but unbreakable. He kept her at his side, his gaze zeroed in on his brother. Her stomach cramped. The tension surged through the room, a chemical electricity that sizzled across her skin.

"As you wish, Your Highness." George bowed,

spared her one cool, scathing look and marched out the way he came in. The door closed in the other room and they were alone again.

She shifted uneasily and glanced down to where his hand held hers. He slid his fingers between hers, interlacing them, and gave her a light squeeze. "He's young and full of himself."

"He loves his brother." Though he shared none of that affection for her. "I should...clean this up."

"No. We can clean it up together after you eat." He lifted her hand to his lips and kissed one knuckle. The warm touch of his lips sent another wave of awareness tingling through her. Her nipples tightened further if that was possible, stinging against the cold bra clinging to them.

He rescued her half sandwich from the other side of the counter and sat it down in front of her.

"Maybe you should go talk to him? He must have flown a long way..."

Shrugging, he plucked a chip from her hair and nibbled it. "Still crunchy." He grinned. "And salty."

"Armand—"

"Do you want a fresh sandwich?" He cut her off.

Sighing, she picked up the half-eaten half sandwich and shook her head. She wasn't hungry anymore, but he held her hand captive and he wanted her to eat. So she ate. He turned and stretched back to open the fridge, still holding on to her while he got them two fresh bottles of water.

"For consumption—not ammunition." He tapped her nose with a finger and she snickered, but the humor failed to gain traction in her soul —not the way their earlier fun had.

"Will you answer my question?"

"Which one?" He had to let her go to open the water bottles, but he didn't move away and she conceded the field on this one, staying right where she was.

"What do I call you?"

He took a long drink of water before tugging his own plate closer. He picked at the sandwich and she thought he might not answer at all. "I told you yesterday, you can call me Charlie."

"And I said Charlie was a lie." She finished the thought and sighed. "I'm sorry I said that—it wasn't very kind."

"No, but it was honest. You are always brutally honest." Sadness crept beneath his words and her heart squeezed. She wanted to wrap her arms around him and chase away the melancholy shrouding him.

She chewed her lower lip, peeling the sandwich apart to pick out the meat. "I don't know if I know how to do this..." She lacked the words to describe the conflict rending through her. She wanted to hug him. She wanted to punch him. She wanted to latch on and never let go. And terrified that this time, walking away would kill her...

He slid a hand behind her neck, familiar, casual—intimate—and so very him. It took very little coaxing for her to look up at him. The gazes crashed together and history seemed to rewind—it was just the two of them. It had always been them against the world—until the day she left him.

"MISS NOVAK, I'm sorry—His Highness is in a meeting." The guard blocked her from accessing the door to Charlie's office.

"Do you know when Charlie—His Highness—will be free?" She grimaced. It hadn't been a full week since they arrived in Norway and she didn't think he'd slept for a moment. Certainly, she didn't see him though she had woken once when he slid into bed next to her—falling immediately to sleep at three in the morning. He'd been gone when she woke again just three hours later.

"I'm sorry, ma'am. I don't." The security guard returned to his position and Anna nodded. Fighting the urge to slide her hands into her pockets, she smoothed her morning jacket. It took her a moment to find a door exiting into a rose garden. The well-manicured lawns were a brilliant shade of green and the roses—they came in all shades from a deep rich golden yellow to a vibrant red.

She wandered through the garden for the better part of an hour before she caught his familiar voice. "One moment, gentlemen."

Charlie strode out the same doors she'd used and crossed the sunny patch of garden to catch her hands in his. "They said you were looking for me. Is everything all right?" He didn't kiss her or do more than grasp her fingers. "I have a meeting with the prime *minister and I don't know how long I'll be. Is it important?"*

*Shaking her head slowly, she murmured. "No, of course not."*

*Lifting her hands to his lips, he kissed her knuckles. "I will find time for us to talk, I promise."*

*Stomach lurching, she forced another smile. "I understand." She didn't—not really. Why hadn't he told her he was a prince? What made him keep the secret from her? Who was this cool, remote man and what had he done with her Charlie?*

*"Your Highness, the car awaits."*

*"I have to go. Have someone take you to the museums. You'll love them." And then he was gone. He didn't return that evening—or at least he didn't until very late. Anna only knew he'd been in her room by the faint scent of his aftershave clinging to the pillow.*

*Each subsequent day followed the same pattern —he'd be tied up for hours in meetings. When he did manage to slip away, they were interrupted time and again—his mother, his brothers, attorneys, guards.*

*"I know you have a lot of questions and I sincerely want to sit down and discuss them all. I have to ask for you to be patient just a bit longer." Three times he'd said nearly the same words to her. It didn't seem to matter how patiently she'd waited, he couldn't make the time.*

*When she woke to a note apologizing that he'd had to go to Belgium, she'd been sick to her stomach. They didn't talk, barely saw each other and she had no idea where she fit into this life.*

*If she even did.*

*When his trip to Belgium turned into a trip to*

*France and then another to England, she'd booked an airline ticket and waited. Anna had to go back to school. Four weeks in Norway, and her finals still awaited her.*

*Her finals. Her diploma. Her future. He didn't have time for her and she was running out of time on the extensions she'd had to file.*

REALITY SANK its ugly claws in her heart and threatened to shred it in half. *She'd* left *him.* *She'd* broken them up.

# CHAPTER 9
# ARMAND

By the time they finished their late lunch, Armand was in a far better mood. A mood George needed to be thankful of, considering his behavior when he'd arrived unannounced. Dressed in fresh clothes, Armand'd left a curiously quiet Anna reading through the foundation history and took the elevator down to the floor beneath the penthouse. George's cool greeting warned of a potential temper explosion, but whereas his younger brother's behavior typically wearied him, today he didn't mind. He rather looked forward to the verbal assault.

He didn't have to wait long.

"Why are you keeping her here?" George poured two glasses of wine. Far too early in the day for heavier spirits, but his brothers never noticed a clock when it came to alcohol. Armand seemed to be the odd man out when it came to that particular habit. The red came from Burgundy; he recognized the vintage as a particular favorite of their mother's.

119

"Manners." Eight years his senior, he would give his younger brother only so much rope.

Like Armand, George had changed out of his food-splattered clothing. But instead of a suit, he wore a polo shirt and slacks. He looked ready for a golf course. The clubs in the corner suggested he planned for one as well. Peterson would discourage him, so Armand left it alone.

"I thought you were with that model—the one with the pixie cut." The younger prince slung himself down on a chair, falling into it rather than sitting.

Armand shrugged, leaning back in his own seat and resting an ankle on a knee. "Does it matter who I'm seeing?" Since Nikole's temper tantrum and threats, he'd been too preoccupied with the discovery of their cousin to concern himself with a new woman.

Anna's arrival complicated everything. Normally, he'd have found a string of eligible, available young women and squired them to a few art openings and theater shows. It would get the press off his back and effectively divide the interest in Nikole's antics. He could hardly begin dating another woman, not even for cover with Anna sharing the penthouse. Hell, he wasn't sure what he wanted to do about the situation, but he wasn't in a sharing mood—not with George.

"No, but Mother is concerned..."

"She is not." He held up a hand and cut his brother's favorite ploy off. The younger prince discovered trotting the mother card out whenever he wanted something from his older brothers worked when he was a child and Armand and Sebastian were in their teens. "In fact, she is in Paris, preparing to attend the Memorial charity ball—a ball you were supposed to escort her to."

George grimaced. "It was all old women and rigid protocol. Not my favorite thing as you can imagine." He drained his wineglass. "Nor is seeing my brother on ACE making a fool out of himself."

"Worried about competition for your most-photographed-inappropriately title?" He swirled the wine in his glass. Anna preferred whites and fruity. He would ask the chef to bring up a selection for their meal that night. She didn't want to drink in the office or at their makeshift lunch—but supper could be a sit-down meal with a white and—

He set the wineglass down and pulled out his phone. Swiping to the text messages, he sent three and looked up to meet George's stony stare.

"When you feel the urge to get around to the point of your unexpected visit, I'll pay more attention to you." The phone in his hand buzzed. Security gave the nod. A second buzz confirmed his chef was on board. The third message remained unanswered.

But he was patient.

George drained his wineglass and bounced up to his feet. He walked over to the bar and refilled it. Fingers drumming against the wood, George didn't sit still.

*It's money...*

"I need an advance on my allowance."

Armand sighed. "What happened?"

"Nothing *happened*. I just need an advance. I was in Monaco one night too many and my luck turned. Then I had to go straight to Paris and Mother's surrounded by the rat pack of societal hangers-on and old guard—" His shoulders rolled in a shudder. "And their far too single daughters and granddaughters."

Armand laughed. The Dickensian predictability of their mother's matchmaking landed on him far more often than not. It was about time George got his taste of it.

"It's not funny." George scowled. "One was thirty-eight and twice divorced."

"Cougars are the rage—or so I hear." He could be sympathetic, but tweaking him was much more fun even if he didn't care for the term.

"According to who? You haven't dated a woman over the age of twenty-five ever."

True. Armand liked his woman too busy and preoccupied with her career to pay attention to his life. The younger they were, the hungrier they were for success, and the less inclined to believe they needed to "land" him. He hadn't even entertained the idea of marriage in years.

Ten to be specific.

"Anyway—" George stabbed a finger in his direction. "With all the fuss, it's costing a bit more for security, so I need an advance."

"You don't pay for your security out of your allowance." Armand rolled the wine around in the glass as though watching the light play off of it.

"You know what I mean..." George returned to the chair opposite Armand's, wine bottle in hand.

"You could mean any number of things, George. I do not presume to interpret your statements for you. You do not pay for your security, so you do not need an advance to cover that." He held up a finger when George opened his mouth to speak. "You do not pay for your travel. You do not pay for your accommodations. You do not spend much time at home, so you do not maintain a regular staff and you fired your valet just a month ago and have not hired a replacement for him. His was the only salary you paid for—so you did not fire the man for incompetence, but because you couldn't afford him."

"You're a real bastard sometimes." His younger brother's shoulders slumped, but the defeat in his tone muted the anger.

"So I've been told. What happened?" Armand sat forward and set his wineglass down. He didn't really want the drink anyway. He studied his brother's expression even as the younger man continued to avoid looking at him directly.

"I made some bad investments—acted on poor advice as you would put it. Now I'm in arrears. I took out a small loan because I thought the return justified it, but—"

Pinching the bridge of his nose, he promised himself he wouldn't yell. "How much?"

"It's not as bad as all that." He set the bottle

and the wineglass down. "It's—just a few thousand dollars."

*Few thousand?* "How few?" Armand clasped his hands together, better not to strangle the younger man.

"An advance is all I need—you can just authorize it—"

"George." One word. His name. A reprimand.

"Two-hundred and fifty thousand dollars."

Armand sat back in the chair and stared. His younger brother rarely shocked him—not after Sebastian's antics all over the globe. A fan of extreme sports, Sebastian took dangerous pursuits to new levels and he periodically went off the grid, leaving everyone to speculate wildly that he'd been killed only to pop up somewhere else. Spoiled, indulged and perhaps even a little petulant, George had been a decent—if lazy—younger brother. He preferred to gamble and drift through his life, only stepping up when it was requested of him.

"Who do you owe the money to?"

"Do you really need the answer to that?" Which meant someone Armand wouldn't approve of—or worse, someone dangerous.

"Fine. I'll pay it. You'll give the name to Peterson and we'll take care of it." He rose from the chair.

"Thank you, it won't happen again and I'll—"

"Go back to school." He cut off the gratitude. Buttoning his coat, he stared at him, unyielding. "You'll enroll this afternoon. Check the schools you're most likely to have an interest in, choose a major, fill out the paperwork, and contact Gretchen with the details. We'll get it taken care of, until then, you will remain here."

"You're serious?" George scrambled to his feet. "Armand, I don't want to go to college."

"I know. You've managed to avoid university for several years now and with legitimate reasons like discovering yourself and blazing your own path. How is that working out for you?" Sometimes being the older brother meant being inclined to cut him some slack. Other times it meant using a mallet. This situation called for the latter rather than the former. George had far too much of the former.

"Is this more of your ex-girlfriend's bourgeois sensibilities? Trying to impress her?" The belligerence wasn't unexpected, no matter how unwelcome.

"Have a care, George. She is a guest, and she will be treated with respect and courtesy—even when she is not present."

"After the way she—"

Armand raised a hand. "George, I will take care of your debt. You will go to school. In the meanwhile, you may stay here until we have sorted your situation out. But under no circumstances will you speak of or *to* Anna in those terms or with that tone again."

Whether it was the solemnity of his statement or the hard stare he gave his brother, it seemed to penetrate. "She dumped you. She walked away and she dumped you."

"She was twenty-two—we both were and

foolish. We thought we knew everything, much as you do now. Do not presume to judge her or myself. I will not tolerate it." The mutiny in his brother's expression threatened to take them into a full-blown argument—one Armand did not want to have. Not when he had so many questions of his own. He was allowed to question her, to wonder why she walked out, why she never tried to reach out to him—why the hell she got engaged to not one man, but two. Yes, he could question it. George could not. His younger brother retreated, however. Armand nodded slowly. "Thank you. Let me know about the schools you're interested in."

"Armand—"

"George, I'm tired. It has been a difficult set of days and I have many issues which need to be seen to." He spared his brother a look.

"I'm sorry." The apology caught him off guard. His brother shoved his hands into his pockets and glanced down. It was hard to forget how many years did separate them, and that George was barely older than he'd been when their father passed away. "I don't mean to be such an ass. I worry about you."

His temper relented. "I appreciate your concern—I do—but focus on your education. You're old enough to be on your own path now. No more...searching—now it's time to find."

"I hate homework."

"Life's little burdens." Armand grinned and left him to it. Outside he punched in Peterson's number and hit the elevator button. "George will give you a name and an account where we need to send a quarter of a million dollars. I want to know everything about the recipient."

"Absolutely. Should I check with his detail?" The men would answer the questions from the security chief, but the point of personal security was also discretion. He wouldn't put the men on the spot yet.

Not unless it became necessary.

"No. For now just wait for the information—and George isn't to leave the tower. He has—" he grinned, "—homework to do."

"Yes, sir. Your Highness, you should also be aware that Prince Sebastian requested the plane to fly him and his detail to Los Angeles."

Armand swallowed an oath unspoken. Pinching the bridge of his nose, he stepped into the elevator. "When is he due to arrive?"

"Two days. I have it from Eduard that his physician gave him clearance to fly." Well, that was something.

"Thank you, Peterson."

"Of course, Your Highness."

The doors closed and Armand hit the button for the penthouse. He had homework of his own...and a story to tell.

~

## ANNA

Had it really been just a little over forty-eight hours before that she sat in the waiting room fuming over the upcoming meeting? Being in the same room again after so many years—what would it be like? What would *he* be like? Did she even know him anymore? She'd put a call through to Chad, and he'd laughed off the press interest. Robert hadn't been available, but she'd spoken to his captain—the only other man who'd known about their engagement—and he'd told her not to worry about anything. Sitting cross-legged in the middle of the bed, surrounded by pamphlets, reports and an illustrated, beautifully photographed guide to the Dagmar Foundation, she faced a far more difficult question.

*Why did I think everything changed?* Thirty-two was far different from twenty-two. Her worldview was broader. Her understanding of need was greater. She appreciated the little things so much more—*so why did I assume he wouldn't?*

She flipped open the guidebook. The interior featured photography as elegant and bright as the exterior. The first page headline read Opening Day Ceremony.

*Of course they held a ceremony.* Armand stood in the center of a larger crowd—he was younger then, much younger. Her Charlie. Dressed in a silky black tuxedo and looking like a million bucks. Her tummy did a flip flop.

Beneath the photo was dated and the caption read: *The Grand Duke Andraste personally cut the ribbon opening the first free clinic for students at the Capital University in Belgium. This international school caters to students from around the globe. The opening of the clinic marks the debut of the Dagmar Foundation, which intends to raise enough funds to cover healthcare for these students and more. The grand duke read a small statement when he cut the ribbon—"everyone deserves an opportunity to fly."*

She slammed the book shut and closed her eyes. The date they opened the clinic was her birthday and the saying—her favorite. She used to tease him that scholarship-funded students should number at least one-third on all campuses because those with money could go wherever they liked and everyone deserved an opportunity to fly.

A tear splashed onto the back of her hand and she swiped at it angrily. Determined, she flipped the book back open. He'd handed her this entire stack with the book on the top because he wanted her to know the foundation's roots. The next page featured an article on the growth of that single clinic and how funds poured in, making it possible to add a dozen more such clinics at European universities catering to all patients—no matter their country of origin.

Filled with similar articles and photographs, the rest of the guide offered a tribute to the Andraste family and the Dagmar fortune being put to work in over thirty-two nations throughout the world. The California scholarship would be the first such project in the United States.

But based on what she read, it wouldn't be the only project. Armand featured in nearly every photo—as often in the background as he was the subject. He dug trenches in Africa to pipe in fresh water. He waded into a rice paddy field in southern Vietnam, offering grants to teachers to travel and teach there.

He walked through a Russian village with a dozen children flocking around him. But it was the images behind him that arrested her heart—men in dark suits and military gear. They all watched him. The prince without a throne dedicated to saving the world—one cause at a time.

She brushed her finger down the photographed cheek. A knock at the door and she jumped, pushing the guide with a guilty jerk. She glanced at the stacks around her, having systematically worked her way through each section of paperwork and lingering only on the guide. She had a lot to straighten to get out of the bed.

"Come in."

The door opened and Armand leaned inside, his polite smile dissolving into amusement at her perch. Letting go of the handle, he leaned against the doorjamb. "Did the stack attack you?"

"No." She made a face. "I got caught up in the reading." She busied herself trying to put the papers back into the organized manner he'd delivered it. She'd taken out several of the charts to match the numbers, however, and that meant they were in the disarray spread around her.

"I was going to invite you to dinner personally since you didn't answer my text." A hint of hurt echoed beneath the words—the barest note of it.

"I turned off my phone." She winced and fished under the stack behind her until she came up with the device and showed him the black screen. "Apparently all the news outlets have the number now. I think they found my Facebook too."

"Ah, the beauty of the Internet. Did you make sure to block your phone number on the social media sites?" He folded his arms, seemingly taking up residence in the doorway.

"Personal data isn't published..." She considered the statement even as she began to say it. She only had an account to begin with because her sister insisted. The whole family used the site, they shared pictures, kept in touch, and occasionally others were added to the circle. She forgot she had it most of the time.

"I'll ask our tech guys to take a look if you'd like. They can correct the settings and block the traffic so you don't have to hide from your family."

Her face warmed and she grimaced. "I'm surprised any of them are talking to me. Penny said Mom chased a half dozen off the farm this morning."

"If they need assistance—" He straightened.

She waved her hand. "No, they have shotguns and the local sheriff is helping. They'll be fine. Brandon's overseas with his Marine unit, so they'd have to go pretty far to bug him, and everyone else is just laughing about it. I have a feeling Penny will be on ACE any day now." In fairness, her sister had stopped chortling about it, but her impulsive behavior remained legendary in their family for a reason.

"You didn't tell them about the threat." It wasn't a question.

Anna shook her head. "No, it would only worry them. The last thing we need is Penny deciding to fly in and rescue me—or worse, everyone else in my family showing up." Her brothers would threaten Armand, and Penny would be all agog at the wealth—but it was her parents. She didn't want to face their disappointment or their determination to "settle" matters. The Novaks were not shy or restrained in any opinion.

"She's in New York—studying at the Metropolitan School of Art, right?"

He knew that? *Of course he knows that...but... why does he know that?*

"Security checks. I wanted to make sure your family was okay." He answered before she could even give voice to the question.

"But you knew before." It was a statement.

"I've...kept track of you through the years." His tone hinted at embarrassment, but his expression proved less revealing.

Her lips pursed. She didn't know whether to be flattered or outraged. The flip-flopping in her belly became a downright hand jive of a dance. "Yes, she's studying contemporary modernism..."

"Aren't they the same thing?" The hesitation tickled her. Did she know something about art that he didn't?

"Well, you would think." She set another stack aside and wondered just how many papers were in this motley pile. She couldn't quite make a path to get off the bed. "But apparently, contemporary refers to the materials and modernism refers to the application."

Armand shook his head slowly. "Not sure I've heard of that—"

"Turning trash into art—people have been doing that for years. Penny just took it a step further. She uses trash as a canvas and then makes it colorful garbage." The corner of her mouth curved. She gave her sister a hard time, but Penny had talent—amazing talent. "And maybe she could do something with this disaster now that I think of it."

"Leave it for now. Dinner is ready and I don't want it to get cold."

"Okay, but if I move, half of this topples onto the floor and it'll be a bigger mess."

He walked across the room and grabbed one of the stacks at the end. Balancing it neatly, he set it on the dresser, then held out his hands. "Stand up and I'll get you out of there."

Her breath hitched. But he waited patiently while her mind whirled that thought around and she bit her lip.

"I won't drop you," he promised solemnly.

*Oh what the hell—if he wanted me that bad, he could have had me on the table yesterday...* Ignoring the twinge of disappointment that he hadn't, she uncurled herself and stood carefully, wincing as one set of papers slid sideways. With a wobbling step, she landed right in his waiting arms. Armand balanced her easily and lifted her over the stacks. She wrapped her arms around his neck and their noses bumped.

Laughter bubbled up and she shook her head. "I remain ever graceful."

He didn't put her down, and although she'd changed into a pair of pajamas, he didn't comment on her clothing either. The green silk pajama set covered everything, but the heat of his body poured through it and set hers on fire. "Yes, you do."

Where her comment was self-deprecating, his sent a thrill skating over her nerves. She bit her lip. They were close—too close—and the hunger she'd glimpsed in his gaze was back. An appetite she shared.

"You said something about food?" They needed to defuse this, right now.

"I did." He leaned closer and inhaled a deep breath. "You showered."

"I know, I'm a bit of a mess." She pushed some of her hair back behind her ear. It fell in curls all around her shoulders. She didn't have her straightener and she didn't want to bother anyone. "And I should probably change."

"No." His gaze swept over her from head to toe. "I think you're perfect."

He started walking and she had to hold on to his shoulders. "But I'm in my pajamas."

"So?" He navigated the hallway and down the three steps into the living room. "It's just us and as you can see, you're dressed perfectly."

The coffee table boasted two large pizzas, a bottle of wine and two glasses. Three fat candles occupied each end table and the lights were dimmed. He deposited her on the sofa and pointed at the television. "It's Wednesday—so it's movie night."

*Movie night.*

The one night a week they'd abandoned their studies, ordered in pizza and raided the mom and pop video store for the latest releases. They always watched by theme—whether that meant horror or romantic comedy. She bit her lip and glanced up at him. He hesitated—waiting.

Waiting for her to say no?

Did she even want to say no?

She slid forward and flipped open the boxes. Spinach and mushroom on alfredo sauce for her and pepperoni and sausage with red sauce for him. Her crust was thin. His crust was thick.

*I can do this. We can do this.* "What's our theme?"

His expression softened and his smile grew. He slid off his shoes and started rolling up his sleeves as he joined her on the sofa. "Action-adventure."

She burst out laughing. "Okay." She grabbed the wineglasses and held them while he opened the bottle and filled each glass halfway—with white wine. White didn't go with the red sauce, but she didn't like reds—wine or sauce. So he'd always gone with white.

"To new adventures." He held his glass up.

"And big explosions." Their glasses clinked together and she took a swallow of the wine. Her stomach rumbled as he lifted up a piece and served it to her on a paper towel. She grinned and nudged him. "Fire it up."

"Yes, ma'am." He pointed the remote at the screen and the sound system echoed with the opening theme music. She leaned back and mirrored his pose, feet up, wineglass in one hand and pizza in the other.

# CHAPTER 10
# ARMAND

The next two days fell into a comfortable pattern. Anna peppered him with questions on safe topics—the foundation, their scheduled launch and the office installation on the fourteenth floor. They avoided the landmines—why she'd left, why he hadn't told her the truth and how much he wanted to rip her clothes off. It worked for them. His security reported two phone calls made—one to Florida and another to the local police station. She'd checked on her ex-fiancés. Neither call lasted longer than five minutes. That she'd made them at all grated.

They ate breakfast together every morning, a silent vigil over coffee punctuated by rustling newspapers as she stole his Italian and French ones first each morning. Her language skills were rusty, but passable. Despite clearing his schedule, a dozen issues cropped up throughout the day that often needed his attention immediately. He hated being pulled away—even from the illusion of being together. Every night, when she headed off to her bedroom, he would brood.

Brood and consider following her. He always nixed the idea. Taking it slow seemed to be working —so slow it would stay. She didn't pull away when he touched her, and she leaned against the back of his chair when he walked her through the spreadsheets for funding. Better still, she touched his arm when pointing out something or arguing her point.

It was all so very civilized—and familiar.

Armand increased the speed on the treadmill and ran faster. His morning runs in the Los Angeles canyons had long since been ixnayed by Peterson and his detail. Too many openings for someone to take a shot at him. The gym helped him curb the need for the run and running took the edge off his need for Anna.

But only barely.

Sweat trickled down his arms and his lungs burned. He pushed himself faster. He couldn't outrun his past, he couldn't outrun his title, so all he could do was burn off the frustration of having her within arm's reach and not touching her.

The door behind him opened and he caught sight of the woman preoccupying his thoughts out of the corner of his eye. She walked in, dressed all in spandex and an oversized Yale sweatshirt. She tossed a towel onto the treadmill next to him and fired it up—to walk.

He forced a grin. "Warming up?"

"They told me I couldn't go to the park." She said it with straightforward calm. Maybe too much calm. "Or the beach. Or my own gym... So here I am..."

She walked steadily and he dropped his run back a notch. The burn in his lungs precluded talking, and he'd much rather talk.

Even if his body preferred other physical activities. *Better to be patient...patient...* Maybe if he chanted it, he could convince his libido to participate in the long-term plan rather than the short-term gains. Sex, however, had never been a problem for them. He missed the feeling of her loose and sated, sprawled against him, and the easy laughter that followed.

The intimacy of being together...

"At least the view here is good." She wasn't looking out the windows to the city below—in fact, she stared at him.

*Is she flirting?* God help him, he wasn't certain. He slowed his pace down another half mile per hour as she began to pick hers up. His lungs expanded in relief, but his pulse continued erratically. Normal considering her nearness.

"It's a good gym. The staff added some of the video game systems with aerobic workouts if you prefer." Not that she ever liked those classes. She did the grunt work with him, running, lifting and stretching. Her form perfect.

"This is good." Her cheeks pinked as she jogged. "You don't listen to music anymore?"

"Too distracting." Not that she wasn't. For the first time he wished they faced a mirror rather than a window—at least he could watch her face without risking tripping by turning his head constantly.

"So what do you do? Run and plan how you will dominate the world?" The words were light and the tone teasing. His mouth curved upward automatically.

"Actually, I try not to think at all." Truth resonated through the words. He tried diligently to block out all distractions—his schedule, his commitments, his loneliness—and just run.

She stumbled a step and put her hand on the bar to catch herself. "Do you want me to go?"

"No." The swift reply left his lips before his brain fully processed her question. The last thing he wanted was for her to go.

"Okay."

They ran in silence. He slowed down and she sped up until their feet hit in perfect rhythm.

"Anna—"

"Charlie—"

They spoke at the same time and laughed as they tripped over each other. "You called me Charlie."

"Yeah." She bit her lip. "You're still Charlie."

The fist locked around his heart loosened and he sucked in relief and hope with the next lungful of air. He missed his Anna. He missed being *her* Charlie.

"I've missed you."

The admission should have knocked him off his stride, but it only served to flood more adrenaline through his system. "I've missed you too." And he wasn't too proud to admit that.

They jogged silently again. The pleasant burn in his thighs ran down to his calves. The steady thump of her cadence next to him pushed him further.

"You were going to say something..." She panted between the words and he nudged the speed a little slower and waited for her to do the same.

"I wanted to say I liked having you here."

"I didn't think I would—like it." Her brutal honesty made its appearance. "I kept thinking that you would hate me and I would be angry and it would—" She grimaced. "I'm oversharing, aren't I?"

"Never." He laughed. "It's one of your more endearing qualities."

"I don't hate you." The words were said so quietly that he actually hit the stop button on the machine and turned to look at her.

She continued to jog until he hit the button on her treadmill.

"Say that again."

Riding the belt backward, she stepped off and put her hands on her hips, gulping air. Sweat gleamed on her face. Her flushed cheeks added to the sparkle in her eyes. "I don't hate you. I don't think...I ever hated you. I told myself I did. A lot." She panted, but she didn't look away.

So many responses came to mind and he frowned. "I didn't like not telling you the truth—about my title. But I never hid who *I* was—am."

Her gaze dropped to her feet and she licked

her lips. "When they showed up that night... When I found out...I was..."

Tucking a finger under her chin, he nudged her gaze back up to him. "Just say it—all of it. I can—I need to hear it."

Two days of skirting Pandora's box was over, maybe they needed to lance the wound and let it pour out. His regrets tangled with a slow, lingering anger that curdled in his gut. But burying it didn't make it go away.

Tongue rubbing against her upper lip, she studied him. "I didn't understand why I didn't know. Why would you keep it so much a secret? Why—why I had to be kept in the dark? And if you could lie about that..."

"What else did I lie about?" He finished the thought for her and nodded. They were fair—if hard—questions. Grabbing his own towel and a bottle of water, he jerked his head toward the mats. "You need to stretch so you don't cramp up."

She trailed after him and it wasn't until they were sitting, legs stretched and the toes of their shoes touching, that he broached the answer. "I didn't tell you—I didn't tell you when I first saw you because I just wanted a date. You were beautiful, sassy and funny—God, you were funny. I liked being around you—even when you said no."

"I only said no for a week," she pointed out, leaning into a stretch over her right knee.

"It was a dreadfully long week." Stalking her schedule, putting himself in her path, learning what she read, what she liked, where she pre-ferred to study—even drinking the terrible java from the coffeehouse she worked in. He followed her stretch and leaned over his left knee, bringing them nose to nose. "And what I wanted was a date—someone who wanted me, not my title. The point of a U.S. university was to fly under the radar. Not announce myself."

He never intended the lie to last. Hell, he didn't intend the lie.

"So why did you call yourself Charlie?" Confusion clouded her gaze and he sighed.

"Anna, I never introduced myself to you as Charlie." He transferred his stretch to his right leg and straightened his foot when she flattened her shoe to his.

"You did, you said—"

"I said," he interrupted smoothly, "'Would you like to get coffee with me after work?'"

She frowned.

"And then you said..."

"'I just served coffee, you think I want to drink it?'" Her wistful smile tied a bow around his heart.

"And I responded, 'Then let me buy you dinner...whatever you want.'"

"I said 'no. I had to study.'" Her lips pursed and she straightened.

"To which I said, 'pizza then—and maybe a bottle of wine...'"

"'No wine. Just water. I said study, not get laid.'" Her lips twitched.

"But you agreed to dinner." He raised his brows.

"Yes, I agreed to pizza. You offered to bring it over to my dorm room and I was in an all-girl dorm and guys weren't allowed, so we met downstairs on the quad and had pizza and water and studied under the tree." She chewed her lower lip.

"Before I left you pulled out a twenty." Exasperation resurfaced at this, as it always did. "You wanted to split the cost of the pizza. That way it wasn't a real date."

She blushed. "You wouldn't take the twenty until I said 'my name is Anna Novak and I don't freeload. A date means promises and I'm not promising you anything—especially when I don't know your name.'"

He nodded slowly and extended his right hand out to her. "'Charles Dagmar, a pleasure to meet you.'"

Anna froze, the smile fading completely from her lips. He watched the memory crash over her and he waited, hand extended. She took his hand in hers, and her fingers trembled. "Hi, Charlie. Nice to meet you."

"And you never called me anything else."

"Charles is your middle name." She gripped his hand tightly.

"Armand was too European—not that the accent wasn't a clue—but Charles westernized my name. Armand Andraste came with an entourage. Charles Dagmar was just a college student." He leaned down and kissed the back of her hand. "But Charlie was the guy lucky enough to get you to say yes to pizza and Charlie was who I wanted to be."

"I named you Charlie." The wonder in her voice had him tugging her hand and she slid forward, rising up onto her knees. She cupped his cheek and stared into his eyes.

"Yes, you did. Charlie was never a lie— Charlie wanted you and—"

The door opened with a hard knock and a cough. "My apologies, Your Highness. But you're needed on the phone immediately. It's the FBI. Your brother's plane landed thirty minutes ago. We expect his arrival at the tower within the next two hours."

He grimaced and closed his eyes, but when he opened them the look in Anna's eyes told him she already retreated. "We are not done with this conversation."

If it were anyone but law enforcement, he would have sent the security guard away. Kissing her hand again, he rose and helped her to her feet. But still he lingered.

"Go." She squeezed his hand. "I'm not going anywhere—except maybe downstairs to meet with Kate and my team."

He tugged her closer again and kissed her— one hard, long, unsatisfying closed-mouth-against-her-lips kiss. "Later," he promised and forced himself to let her go and follow the guard out.

∾

## ANNA

"Earth to Anna, come in, Anna." Becca Sampson knocked on the desk. The recent renovations gave everyone a cubicle to work in, but the setup was a large circle so no one was actually behind a wall. Kyle stood just inside the entrance and a second guard was a few feet away. Despite her staff gaining security clearance, she would not be alone on any floor save the penthouse—and she just skipped asking them why that was.

She knew the answer.

Charlie wanted privacy with her and privacy they would have. A far cry from those days in Norway when she hadn't managed to get five minutes with him without interruption.

"Yes? Sorry, I'm...distracted."

"If I were dating a prince, I wouldn't be working so you're already three steps ahead of me." Becca breezed across the subject and laid out a brochure. "This is the mock-up I'm working on, but we need to talk to some of the kids that were handpicked to receive the first round of scholarships. I think we should get photographs and stories from each of them and feature them prominently in the center of a series of brochures."

Anna rubbed the back of her neck and studied the layout. They broke down the benefits of the scholarship program on one side and the requirements for application on the other. "We need this to be more prominent." She tapped the line about ideals and goals. "Grades will factor into where they go to school, not whether they qualify for the scholarship. Move the GPA requirement to last on the list."

"You think a C-average student is really going to apply?" Becca was young, but her cynicism finely honed.

"I think a C-average student should absolutely want to apply and not feel that his or her grades automatically disqualify them. Some kids don't do well in high school—whether it's their friends, their teachers, or their circumstances. You take that same group of teens and you put them in college with even one person saying 'I believe in you' and they thrive. That's what every single one of these brochures has to deliver—the promise that we believe in them." She exhaled. It bothered her when her staff, even those who believed in the opportunity, limited the vision to the definition of who "deserved" it. Derrick Milton had proven in every way to be a poster child for this effort—he didn't think he was worthy, but she'd made a point of emailing him and calling him since they'd spoken. If someone told him enough times he deserved the chance to fly, maybe he would begin to believe it too.

"But they still have to qualify, which means it's more than the application process—they have to be approved." Becca chewed her lip and studied the layout. "That's why I think we need to really sell this based on those we've prequalified and made our offers to. You use their names, their stories, their backgrounds and you'll have kids going, 'hey, that girl's just like me' or 'I am doing the same things this guy is doing.' They want someone to believe in them, but they aren't going to buy that at face value and as Pollyanna as you can be, you know that."

And the only reason she dragged Becca with her from the last project was her blunt approach to marketing faith.

"Okay, let's get some phone calls made. We've got ten offers out there for the first round of scholarships and only two have accepted. I'm betting the others don't believe it's real or there's another issue." She turned her chair around. "Tony?"

"Already on it." He waved at her with the phone in his hand. "I'm waiting to talk to Darnell Jamison's foster mom."

"Great. Good work, Becca."

"Yep." Becca left the mock-up on her desk and went back to work. Anna turned back to her screen and pulled up the initial funding spreadsheet. They could afford to offer twenty scholarships immediately. They earmarked ten based on questionnaires sent to one hundred high schools and cross-checked with those sent to all the social worker offices in the same areas. Pooling the data helped them identify the ten most worthy and needy candidates. Students with promising futures deemed least likely to go to college because of financial concerns—and in the top two cases because of conflicts within their foster care situations.

Twenty scholarships.

It was a small start. But they dedicated the

rest of the money toward fundraising with the goal of increasing that number ten times for the next autumn. The Dagmar Foundation pledged ten million—a check she would receive on Friday during the charity event at the concert hall. The check, of course, was only symbolic. The funds would be transferred electronically. The move was to encourage others to donate as well—the first unofficial fundraiser for the Princess Alyxandretta Dagmar scholarship fund.

The numbers blurred on the screen and she blinked rapidly. A tear slid down her cheek and splashed against the keyboard. Dabbing at her eyes, she frowned. Sniffling, she pulled her purse out of the drawer and fished out a tissue. It wasn't the first wave of tears to assault her that day and it probably wouldn't be the last.

Forcing herself to focus, she stared at the spreadsheet again and saved it as a different file. Adding the prospective ten million and creating columns where the number increased in five-hundred-thousand increments, she began to calculate operating costs and scholarship disbursements. In a separate worksheet, she checked the expected increase in college tuition over the next five years.

The average student entering a four-year state university in their home state could expect to spend twenty thousand dollars annually—and that included food and residency. The current scholarship would allow for two years, but not the full four. Specialized schools would double that amount and a for-profit institution could triple it. The words wavered every few minutes and she dabbed her eyes again, thankful she skipped any mascara after her workout this morning.

Charlie.

She dubbed him Charlie. He told her his last name and his first, but beyond that first date he had always been Charlie. Her crazy, off-the-wall, terrifically romantic Charlie. Moving in together at the end of their sophomore year made sense. They were always together and it saved money for both of them.

She paused mid-column. No. It had saved money for her. Charlie never said it saved anything for him and that wasn't why he made the offer. Money never came up in conversation unless she brought it up.

Then it had usually involved her saying no to something because it was too expensive. Squeezing her eyes shut. *Idiot. Idiot. Idiot. Idiot.*

More tears fell and she had to keep her back to Becca and Tony when they headed out at four so they wouldn't see her red-rimmed eyes. Kate paused to drop a printout on her desk, but Anna didn't look up and after a moment she moved on. Anna stayed planted at the desk, determined to finish her projections so that if it came up at dinner, they could brainstorm fundraising ideas.

*Because fundraising is safer than talking about how stupid you are...*

A dull ache formed behind her right eye and began to pound in time with her pulse, but she kept at it. Flipping screens, she looked up different schools and their current tuition rates, and programming alternative columns to increase the rates by ten percent per year. The graphic representation showed that at bare minimum students would need about sixty thousand dollars to complete a four-year degree at a non-specialized school while for-profits and specialized universities would cost upward of one hundred and fifty thousand for the same four years.

The bleak results didn't improve her rapidly darkening mood. The phone on her desk rang and with everyone else gone, she answered it automatically. "Alyxandretta Dagmar Scholarship Fund, Anna Novak speaking. How may I help you?"

"Miss Novak. Thank you for answering. This is Lilly Lymon with the *Evening Star, London* news. We were calling for your comment on the recent engagement announcement released an hour ago."

*Damn press, and we just changed the number.* "I'm sorry, Ms. Lymon, I'm afraid I have no comment." She went to hang up the phone, but the woman rushed onward.

"None at all regarding the engagement of the Andraste prince to Nikole?"

The headache behind her eye became an ice pick striking right through her heart.

"No." Miraculously, her voice remained completely calm. "None at all."

She hung up the phone and stared sightlessly at the computer screen.

After hitting two buttons to save the work,

she stood up and walked past the guards and into the bathroom. Her red-rimmed eyes hurt and the surge of temper flooding through her aggravated her more. She pulled out her cell phone and turned it on. It took a minute to boot up and she ignored the incoming texts and waiting voice-mails to flip to the web browser. Plugging in the name *Nikole*, *news* and *prince*, she let it search and washed her face. By the time the screen populated, she saw several reports—all filed in the last sixty minutes—announcing Nikole's "secret engagement," to the Grand Duke Andraste.

Torn between outrage and amusement, she started laughing.

Nikole let the details "slip" during a recent party on a Mediterranean yacht. She immediately retracted the statement with a coy wink and a nod.

Nikole. Not Charlie. Not his family.

They weren't engaged. Pleased, she shut her phone off and ran her fingers through her hair. She exited the bathroom and her heart hitched again.

Sebastian perched on the corner of her desk —like George, Sebastian was also a younger version of her Charlie. His exploits had earned more headlines than his brother. Pale beneath his tan, the prince stood with a faint grimace at her approach. "Hello, Anna."

To her utter surprise, he caught her hands and drew her close to press a kiss to each of her cheeks. "Hello, Sebastian."

It had been a decade since the last time she

saw him anywhere beyond a news article. Of all the people she'd met during her sojourn in Norway, Sebastian had shown her the greatest amount of kindness and insisted she call him by his given name. Canting his head to the side, he studied her puffy eyes. "Are you well?"

Plastering on a smile, she resisted the urge to sniff. "I think I should be asking you that question. Weren't you injured recently?"

He waved off the concern. "I've done more damage on a ski trip in Switzerland." Despite the airy words, lines of strain tightened the corners of his eyes.

"I'm afraid Charl—" she bit off the name, "Armand is not here."

Sebastian glanced over at Kate, who had no choice but look at them since her desk faced Anna's. "Do you mind if we talk somewhere more privately?"

Kate rose from her desk and pointed to the eastern wall. "They finished the conference room today, Anna, and I'll take care of this last spreadsheet if you like."

"Thank you." Anna followed Sebastian and noted the faint stiffness to his gait. He might have dismissed his injury, but he couldn't disguise the physical effect with an expensive suit or easy smile. Kyle and a man she didn't recognize followed both of them, but neither made any attempt to join them in the conference room.

Sitting, so Sebastian would do the same, Anna studied Armand's younger brother. It was uncanny how much he and his brother could be twins, but the differences were there. A scar high on his right cheekbone, an easier smile, and his eyes didn't have the same lingering sadness or depth—as though the weight of the world rested upon him.

"I fear I should go directly to the point of this visit." The grave tone sent a warning shiver up her spine. George made it plain he did not want her around, going so far as to avoid her completely. She hadn't missed his very deliberate snub in the hallway the day before when they'd approached from opposite directions. He'd simply turned his back on her and gone back the way he came.

Clasping her hands together, she lifted her chin. Braced for it, she waited. "Go ahead."

"I owe you a profound apology, one I do not think I can ever make amends for." He sat forward in his chair, hands together on the edge of the table. His aristocratic bearing failed to hide the distress lurking beneath the surface. "I truly believed that it would take certain maneuvers to undo the great injustice of the past. Sometimes, dramatic solutions are called for... I am saying this very poorly."

"I'm sorry, I'd have to agree. What great injustice?" Unable to ignore the upset radiating off him, she covered one of his hands.

"You and Armand. The two of you were once happy. Our family, our way of life—it can be overwhelming. I recognize that." Desperation flickered around the edges of his words. He turned his hand beneath hers, capturing her fingers. "But you two were very good together. I do not believe he has ever gotten over you and my only defense lies in wanting my brother to be happy. He can very hidebound—very restricted by responsibility. I didn't think he would ever make the move on his own."

Anna frowned, trying to follow Sebastian's rather circuitous dialogue, and the dull thud of the headache behind her eyes wasn't helping. "I'm sorry, Sebastian. I don't know what you're talking about."

He sighed and glanced down, an expression vaguely resembling shame on his face. "I called them."

"Called who?" Utterly mystified, Anna fought her scowl. It was like having a conversation with Penny when she didn't want to admit something out loud.

"The press." The younger prince grimaced. "I called the press and told them you and Armand were together again—"

"You did what?" Armand's furious voice sliced across the stunned silence.

# CHAPTER 11
# ARMAND

R age burned like acid in Armand's veins. He took in the scene with one glance from Anna's red-rimmed eyes to the way his younger brother held her hands—comforting and familiar. Too damn familiar.

Sebastian jerked to his feet, releasing her in the process. "Armand, I—"

"Silence." For once, his brother did exactly what he told him to do.

"Charlie." Anna stood. "Sebastian was just—"

"Anna, if you will excuse us, Johnson can return you to the penthouse."

"I will not excuse you," she sputtered. She paced toward him and he got a better look at the puffiness around her eyes—the redness. "I'm a part of this."

Coldness fisted in his gut. George. The FBI. The death threats. Anna's reticence. Now Sebastian. His world threatened to spin out of control, and it was his responsibility to see to it all. It had always been his responsibility. Dabbling in the game of Charlie was an amusing pastime, but he'd made the mistake of believing in the fairy tale. "Actually, it is a family matter. Now please excuse us."

Anna stiffened. "Charlie—"

"Enough, Anna." An aggravating day with the FBI's team of analysts and his own security forces had left Armand in a foul temper. The FBI further rocked him with news about the discovery of a device in Anna's house that could have detonated her gas line. Yes, they'd removed it and kept it quiet, but their actions didn't change the vigor of the threat. Richard's texts about Nikole's ill-advised slip had served to only fuel his anger. He'd gone directly to the fourteenth floor to find Anna. The last thing he wanted was *another* battle with her—not when they'd come so close to a breakthrough earlier in the day—before his life, his *duty* intervened. Now, Sebastian's betrayal, it was just too much.

He stared at his brother, but directed his words to Anna. "*Go.*"

Without another word, she strode out of the room and the door slammed behind her.

"You didn't have to be such an ass to her," Sebastian began, but swallowed whatever else he might have said when their gazes clashed.

"If not for the gravity of your injury, I'd break that nose of yours and shove your teeth down your throat." He might yet. It took every ounce of his self-control to keep his hands at his sides and not fisted. Only a handful of weeks before, a knife had been thrust between Sebastian's ribs and punctured his lung—had his bodyguard not reacted so swiftly... Armand ended the path of that thought. "Explain exactly what you did."

Sighing, his brother clasped his hands behind his back. "When you called me to ask for my advice, it was the first time in years I heard hope in your voice. Hope and desire—for something other than a new project for orphans." His brother sighed, his face twisting as though he struggled with the words. "You haven't been the same since she left."

"I did not ask for your analysis of my mental condition or my phone call. I was on the other end of the receiver." Apparently calling his brother had been a mistake. He'd thought Sebastian might understand the conundrum—as second in line, Sebastian's education and upbringing had closely matched Armand's own. Like him, Sebastian did not form attachments and he dutifully went where the family sent him —save for his little rebellions. Rebellions he as the second son had been allowed. "Why did you call the press?"

"Because you're turning into your title, and you're getting colder. You love that woman, you're just too damn stubborn to see it. If you'd swallowed your pride for five minutes—"

"Enough." Armand sliced his hand through the air. Everyone wanted to argue with him. "You... George... Neither of you learn. Go have your injury seen to and no more phone calls."

"I came to apologize to her. I didn't consider the danger or how badly the press would react."

"Of course you didn't. But we did not play our parts in your little Machiavellian farce." Sliding his hands into his pockets, Armand walked over to the windows and stared down at the city. The fourteenth floor was closer to the street and yet it felt very far removed from the frenzied pulse of life traveling beyond the walls of the tower.

After a long moment, his brother sighed, the door opened and he left.

"Your Highness." Peterson must have been waiting for their exit.

Not turning around, Armand closed his eyes. "Yes?"

"Miss Novak is secure in the penthouse."

"Thank you."

"Agent Fielding called, they wanted to clarify that they have officially identified another player in the latest threats against Miss Novak." Latest threats—four more had arrived over the course of the week. Each promised an escalation in violence.

"More than the magazine reporter?" A disgruntled magazine reporter working for a local periodical had attempted to trade on a professional relationship with Anna and she'd snubbed him by failing to respond. According to the agents, when questioned, the man pled guilty to felony threat and third-degree stalking. He'd also lost his job. Two others had been discredited as copycats. The fourth, however, had been as credible as the first. And far more violent—including three photographs of Anna taken at different points during the week as she visited potential scholarship recipients. Each one had featured her security.

They'd included crosshairs, distance references and a one-word note: *anytime*.

"Yes, in addition to adding Yuri Markov—the businessman Prince George took the loan from—they have information from a credible source citing political unrest in Belaria."

Turning around, Armand stared at Peterson. Belaria, a tiny footnote of a country straddling a landmass between Russia, Hungary and the former Czechoslovakian Republic. The independent Slavic nation established a formal government after the collapse of the U.S.S.R., but prior to the revolution it had been an ancestral home to Russian Czars, filled with noble estates and huge tracts of hunting land for young princes to cut their teeth safely.

"Good God, why there?" The family maintained few interests in the region due to the unrest. Even his cousin Francesca, with her peculiar habits for visiting hot spots, avoided the region.

"It seems they've developed a multiparty system over the last five years. In the last several months, one has truly begun to gain a foothold over the others." Peterson's implacable expression kept his emotions in check, but Armand dreaded what he was about to say. "A royalist party that has named you their titular figurehead."

The headache behind his right eye became a red-hot poker of pain digging into his brain. "Find out what you can. Keep Sebastian and

George on lockdown—and reach out to my mother's security forces, as well as the Graces." His aunt—his father's sister—and her husband were likely in the United States, but their three daughters were more likely in Europe.

Peterson walked him to the elevator, they rode up to the security level where Peterson exited and if not for the camera, Armand would have leaned against the wall.

*Sebastian* called the press. Of all the brash, impulsive, foolhardy things to do...

On the penthouse floor, Johnson waited outside the door, an unusual deviation from protocol. He lifted a brow at the man and the bodyguard straightened. "Your Highness."

"Is Miss Novak secure?"

"Yes, sir."

"Then why are you still here?" He didn't bother to disguise his annoyance. To access the penthouse required the security station to allow the elevator to travel to the floor in the first place. Security did not remain on this floor unless expressly invited—not with Anna in residence. He valued his privacy—what little he could manage —especially with her.

"Miss Novak was not in the best frame of mind, sir. I thought it prudent to be available." If Armand wasn't mistaken, Johnson's attitude held a firm note of disapproval and verged on insubordinate.

"I will take care of Miss Novak. Good night, Johnson."

The man bowed slightly, and Armand waited

until the elevator doors closed and he descended before opening the door to his apartment. Anna stood in the middle of the living room, arms folded with cool hostility in her gaze. He'd had a whole speech prepared on the drive over, and he'd wanted to soothe any feathers ruffled by Nikole's ridiculous actions. But the incident with Sebastian had pushed it out of his head.

"Before you say anything..." He needed to explain. "I have no idea what Nikole was thinking when she made that statement. But it is categorically not true." He could only hope she believed him.

"You're not engaged?"

"Of course not." He frowned. "I understand it was difficult to hear."

"Not really." Anna shook her head. "Not even a little. If you'll excuse me, Your Highness, I'm sure you have other royal business you need to attend to."

"Anna—" He caught her arm, and she glared at him. "I'm *not* engaged."

"Maybe you should be—maybe she wouldn't care if you ordered her around like a dog. I, however, do." Jerking her arm free, she made it three steps before spinning around. "But you know what's the worst part?"

Impassive, he stared at her. "I am certain you will tell me."

"You don't know, do you?" Shock replaced the upset in her expression.

"Anna, I'm tired and I have a headache. It has been an incredibly challenging day. On any other

163

occasion, I would revel in letting you sharpen your tongue against me, but if you could simply tell me what it is that has upset you in a rational manner, we can deal with it and move on."

Her mouth opened, but no sound came out. Her eyes hardened and heat seemed to shimmer in her gaze. With a small scream of frustration, she whirled and stalked down the hall. The door to her bedroom slammed shut a moment later. Rubbing a hand against his forehead, he decided against following her. Letting her cool off seemed the prudent choice.

## Anna

IN HER ROOM, Anna had to fight against opening the door to slam it again. She settled for kicking the edge of her bed and tears sparked in her eyes at the punishment to her toes. *Of all the arrogant... pigheaded...overbearing...*

She let out another little scream and clenched her fists. How the hell could he dismiss her—order her out of a room—and then act like he'd done nothing wrong? Fuming, she slammed into her bathroom, showered. He'd dismissed her—effectively told her to get out.

*Bastard.*

Bracing her hands against the tile, she bent her head under the spray and ignored the tears running down her cheeks. *Why?* He'd been angry with his brother. Of course he'd been angry. Sebastian told the press they were together. The burning in her eyes doubled and she swallowed a sob. *"You two were good together. I do not believe he's ever gotten over you."*

Could have fooled her. She washed her hair twice and then leaned against the tile, letting the hot steamy water drown out her tears. Charlie never got angry. In all their years together, she'd never seen him behave...

*Like what? A prince? A man who expects his orders to be obeyed?* When they were together, he'd been her Charlie. Her best friend. Her soul mate. *God, I am so stupid.* How could she continue to think of him that way? Hadn't that little episode demonstrated beyond a shadow of a doubt that he wasn't Charlie?

*So why then did he come to see me? He didn't know Sebastian was there—I saw the shock on his face.* Nikole's ridiculous statement to the press had been the first thing he'd brought up. *So why throw me out...?*

Because Charlie didn't lose his temper and he'd been furious. Anna straightened and shut off the water. Controlled. Everything about him was so controlled. Every word deliberate, every action —every reaction—he moderated them. He behaved in all things...

"Like a prince. Like he's on display and he is very aware of the impressions he makes." Even to her. He'd been furious with his brother and he wanted to yell at him. That said, he also hadn't wanted to yell in front of her. After climbing out of the shower she toweled off swiftly, pausing only to finger comb her hair.

Grabbing the first thing she found in the dresser, she dragged on an old sweatshirt and a pair of shorts. She had to talk to him—clear all of it up. Her courage flagged at the door, and she hesitated.

What if he didn't want to talk to her?

Indecision rippled through her. Pacing over to the bed, she picked up the phone and dialed her sister.

"Hello, Blocked Number, you have reached the residence of 'what the hell do you want?' You have three seconds to answer or I hang up..."

"Good evening to you too." Laughter escaped, she forgot that the private penthouse wouldn't have caller ID. She should have used her cell phone.

"Well, hello, stranger. You sound suspiciously like my sister, but that can't be. She's been too preoccupied with recapturing the past to call and let me know she's still alive." The snarky tone belied the real concern echoing beneath the words.

The horrible rocks settling on her chest dislodged at Penny's voice. "I have been busy and I am sorry, I would say you could've called me—"

"Oh, I did, but calling you requires your cell phone to be on and since I ring straight through to your very full voicemail, I'm guessing it hasn't been." Water echoed behind Penny's words followed by a metallic thud. "Okay, teakettle is on.

I've got a soothing blend of chamomile waiting for me—give me the deets. What's going on?"

"We've set up the fourteenth floor for the scholarship fund." She grasped on to the relative normalcy of it all. She needed it. "Kate—she's the new assistant is a Godsend—she's more organized than I am. Becca's got some great design plans for the brochure. I have some more numbers to crunch and it could take a while to make a real impact, but I think we have a lot of potential."

She rolled onto her back and stared at the texture of the ceiling. Penny was silent for a long moment. "And?"

"And what?" Anna fidgeted, sitting up and balancing the phone between her ear and shoulder. She'd hoped a shower would help the too-tight feeling of her skin.

"Helloooo—hot ex-boyfriend—hot, *royal* ex-boyfriend. What's up with you and Charlie?" The kettle whistled in the background.

Shrugging, she scrambled to catch the phone when it fell and grimaced as her foot impacted the edge of the bed. "Dammit."

"Hey, you called me," Penny pointed out.

"No, I hit my foot on the bed." Again.

"Oh, are you in bed with him right now? Wait—if you're in bed with him, why the hell are you calling me?" Her sister's tease didn't help the cramp twisting her insides up.

Scrubbing a hand against her face again, Anna sighed. "We're not in bed together."

"Bummer. Why not?" She slurped her tea noisily and Anna stared up at the ceiling.

"Penny, I didn't call you to talk about Charlie." *Liar.* "How's school going?"

"It's fine and boring. You did too call me to talk about Charlie—I can hear the tension in your voice. I bet your nostrils are flaring and your mouth has that pinched, sucked-on-a-lemon look to it. So, what did he do?" Blithe, carefree Penny didn't stand on ceremony with anyone and certainly had no concepts of privacy.

"Does it really matter?" *He's breaking my heart and I don't even know why. We're not really together and then it feels like we are. How can this stranger be so damn familiar?* Her life was not this bag of insanity—she liked everything in its place. She kept it in place.

"Hey, if I need to fly to Los Angeles and kick his royal tushy, I will head to the airport right now. So come on, sis—let the anxiety out. It has to be giving you heartburn by now."

The acidic bile in the back of her throat confirmed her sister's assessment, but she didn't need to tell her that. The sweatshirt was too hot, and her skin itched. After rolling off the bed, she walked back over to the drawers and rummaged through them—she wanted something of her own. It seemed a number of the "guest" clothes had been intermingled with hers. "It's nothing like that."

"So what is it like? You know I'm not going to stop asking and if you don't tell me, well, I'll just call Mom and tell her he broke your heart again and she'll tell Tommy and Dad and—"

"You do realize it's rude to blackmail your sister, right?" She fished out a worn, three-sizes-too-big T-shirt and stared at it. The simple black shirt with the silver Yale on the front was Charlie's favorite—he'd worn it everywhere. When she returned to the States and arranged to move out of their apartment, it ended up in her boxes —probably shuffled into their mixed laundry. She'd never returned it. She always meant to do it, but sometimes after a particularly horrendous day, she would slip it on and remember.

*When did I become such a sap?*

"Pfft. It's not blackmail when you're related." Penny intruded, but Anna traded the sweatshirt and shorts for the T-shirt before answering.

"Oh?"

"Nope. It's leverage. So, spill. What's going on with you and Charming Charlie?"

Anna's eyes widened. "Oh my God. Do not call him that."

"I kind of like it, it's got a good ring to it and it comes with bling—heh heh." Penny chortled, but her laughter was short-lived. "And stop being so evasive. What's wrong?"

"I don't know. Nothing. Everything. I started this week like any other on a new project, one hundred percent focused on making it a success. Now I'm living with a man that is so damn familiar it hurts and I'm not even sure I ever really knew or know now." She exhaled, sitting on the edge of the bed. The little girl lost was not her—

nor was this horrible loss of options. "Maybe I should suggest I move to a different place, get out from underfoot. I don't have to be here to be secure and I can't think this is making it any easier to say we're not involved when—"

"One. You're involved. Two. You're babbling. Three. What happened?" Penny's voice sharpened, all of the playfulness evaporating.

"We kissed." There, she said it.

"Sweet." Excitement bubbled in Penny's voice. "Who kissed whom?"

"Does it matter?" She flopped against the pillows. Her lips tingled when she thought about their kisses.

"Of course it matters. Did he kiss you? Did you kiss him?"

"The first time—"

"First time? You've been holding out on me, that's multiple kisses."

Anna let out an exasperated huff. "It's not like that."

"Uh-huh."

Anna groaned. "Penny, you're killing me here."

"Killing you? You're the one holding on to all the juicy details."

"He kissed me first." She was never going to get her shut up about it until she answered. "But he was mad—I think."

"Why do you think he was mad?" Bless her, instead of the a-ha Anna had expected, Penny sounded quiet, thoughtful.

"Because he kissed the hell out of me and walked away." Her body hummed. The heat spreading from her face to her chest and across her belly—she would have made love with him right then and right there, but he walked away.

"Okay, angry kisses are good." Relief bumped her voice up a notch. "That's untapped passion aching to be released. And the next kiss?"

"Well, technically...he kissed me again." Did the gym kiss really count? The firm affection in his manner and his lips left the butterflies in her stomach in an uproar.

"That you have doubt means you need to give me more details..."

She sighed. Penny really was impossible. "We were working out and talking, he had to go. He gave me a quick kiss because he had to go."

"With or without tongue?"

"None of your business."

"Definitely means without. Go on." Something squeaked in the background, followed by a clicking noise and a long inhale.

"Penny, are you smoking again?"

"Nope." She blew out a breath. "And we're not talking about me, we're talking about you and Charming Charlie. So we have one and a half kisses on his side. What's next?"

She promised herself to get after her sister later. "Next Nikole let it slip in some interview that she and Charlie were engaged..." Even though she'd realized it wasn't true, the words had hurt.

"That bitch." God love a sister who immediately championed her cause. Anna summarized the rest—Sebastian's confession, Armand's dismissal and her confusion over it all.

She didn't know whether they were coming or going. Less than a week ago, he was still a relic of her past—a huge relic—but that was where she kept him, safe and secure in a memory box that she could take out late at night. But now, he was here in her present, so alive, virile and strong.

"What was I supposed to do?"

"What do you want to do?"

*Kiss him. Slap him. Scream. Leave. Stay.*

*I don't want a death threat forcing him to keep me close when clearly we are better off apart.*

But she said none of that. She hadn't told anyone—particularly her family—about the threats, she didn't want her family to know. "I don't know." Anna sighed. "I don't know what I want. We were done—dead and buried."

"Bullshit." The flat tone cut off her self-pity. "You two haven't been over since the day you came home."

"Penny!"

"No, you know it was one thing when you were moping around and refusing to talk about it. Everyone danced on eggshells because you looked like hell. You missed him so bad, *my heart* hurt. But it was your business and we all took your side because he lied—but Anna, come on, you're smarter than this. You want something, you go after it."

"He's ordering me around like I'm some servant, that doesn't say he wants me, Pen."

"No, it says you burned him and he doesn't want to be burned again." She didn't mince her words. "You know what your problem is?"

"I'm guessing you're going to tell me." Were they really sending each other mixed signals?

"Yup. You think too much. You forget that half of a relationship is how good the other person makes you feel—and Charlie makes you feel great. You've sounded more like you in this last week with all the insanity than you have in years. You know what your other mistake is?" Penny continued without waiting for an answer. "You're on the phone with me instead of going out there and making your prince come."

Anna sat straight up. "Penny!"

"Yeah, you were thinking it, I just said it. So now I'm going to do you the best favor of your life. I'm going to hang up now—"

"Penny."

"I hear an orgasm calling your name. Ta-ta for now!" The phone clicked in her ear and Anna stared at it. Every time she thought her little sister couldn't shock her more, she dispensed her own peculiar blend of wisdom and snark.

She could sit here and continue to feel sorry for herself or she could beard the lion in his den. Anxiety twined around the fear in her gut. What if he really didn't want her anymore?

*Then I'll know—we'll both know—and we can stop hurting each other once and for all.*

Leaving the phone in the middle of the bed,

she crossed to the door and headed out. This called for a bottle of wine and two glasses.

*Time to rip the Band-Aid off...*

## CHAPTER 12
# ANNA

Padding barefoot down the hallway, she glanced in the kitchen and living room before traveling across the hardwood floors and rich Venetian rugs to the archway that led off into an unexplored wing of the penthouse. Charlie kept an office in the suite—he must, because twice this week he retired to that office to take calls. He never invited her back to it. But with a bottle of wine in one hand, two wineglasses in the other and her courage on her sleeve, she planned to invite herself.

*What if he tells me to get out? Again.*

She slid to a halt. Grumbling about her own lack of courage, she pushed onward. Better to know than to wait, wonder or hope. She'd waited for ten years—she hadn't meant to, definitely hadn't planned to or even realized—until he railroaded himself back into her life. If she didn't want him here, she wouldn't have agreed to stay, to work so closely to him, and she sure as hell wouldn't have wanted to kiss him.

At the door to his office, she raised her hand to knock. Deciding against that, she juggled the wine bottle and glasses and opened the door. He sat behind his desk and his gaze alighted on her immediately. Pleasure flared in his eyes and his mouth parted, but she held up a finger to halt his words.

"We need to talk—and by that, I mean really talk. No more dancing around it, no more polite deflections." The carpet in his office was like silk against her feet and the cool air brushing her legs reminded her she was hardly dressed professionally, but she plowed onward. Setting the wine bottle and glasses down, she flattened her hands against the desk. "I propose that for the next twelve hours we each give the other a pass. We can ask anything we want, answer it all—honestly—no harm, no foul. We clear the air between us."

Charlie leaned back in his chair and steepled his fingers together. His eyebrows lifted in silent inquiry.

"Yeah, that's...it. That's my proposal." She chewed her lip, the nervous fluttering in her belly turning into a full-fledged stampede.

The moment of truth...

"Okay. Richard, if you wouldn't mind excusing us..." Charlie looked around her. Mortification flamed through Anna and she straightened up, her current state of undress adding to the embarrassment. Turning slowly, she found Richard standing at the minibar in the office, a tumbler in his hand.

"Hello, Richard." She gathered together the shreds of her dignity. "I'm sorry, I didn't realize you were there."

"Clearly." The droll humor in his smile didn't make her feel any better. "And I agree, Armand. I'll call you tomorrow."

He sailed toward the door in three quick strides, pausing long enough to give her a reproving look. "It's good to see you again, by the way. Cut the big guy some slack..."

Lifting both brows, she kept the mild irritation at his advice in check. "Tell me, Rick. When did he tell you?"

Richard cut his glance from her to Charlie. She didn't turn to follow the purely silent pulse of communication transmitting between the two. Whatever he saw in the prince's face satisfied him. "End of freshman year."

"Okay, so three years before I found out and he actually *told* you." She let him chew on that.

"But I didn't run." Rick's voice went low and it was damn near a murmur.

Anna sucked in a breath. "No. He also didn't ignore you."

Behind her, she could hear Charlie shifting at his desk, but neither she nor Richard spoke any louder. "No, but *I* didn't ignore you either—you could have called me."

True. She could have and maybe Richard could have helped—Charlie, her, someone. "I'm sorry I didn't call, but it wasn't about you. He and I should have been able to do this without you running interference. So..."

"So I'll shut up and mind my own business. Give him hell, Anna. But don't run away from him this time." Richard's sober expression gave way to a quiet smile and he glanced around her to Charlie, raising his voice at the same time. "You're on your own, buddy." And with that, he was gone.

"He always was the smart one." She turned back to Charlie and pursed her lips. "Sorry for bursting in, I should have knocked."

"No—you shouldn't have. You were beautiful in your determination. Fierce... I liked it." But he stayed behind the desk, so she grabbed a chair and pulled it forward. The fabric seat was cool against her bare legs.

"And my proposal?"

"It's dangerous, Anna." Charlie sat forward now and reached for the wine bottle. He studied the label but made no move to open it. "You want us to—how did you phrase it? Stop dancing around? Be honest?"

"Yes." The nerves curled through her again, but her little sister was right and it was time—and frankly, she wanted it to be time. "I'll understand if you don't want to. You know, maybe I won't understand it, but I will respect it. But I can't keep kissing you, crying over you, and having all these questions and feelings and memories and wondering what we're doing or why we're doing it."

His jaw tightened when she said cry, but she held her ground. "What if you hear something you don't like? Or I do?" He didn't challenge the premise, instead clarifying the terms. She could appreciate that.

"No walking out. No walking away. We stay here—we check our tempers at the door and we talk." Scooting to the end of the chair, she put her hands on the desk.

"And if we fight?" His gaze shuttered, his expression turning remote. She courted not only Charlie, but the prince who'd dismissed her earlier.

"Then we fight. But a fight doesn't mean the end—we used to be able to fight and not hurt each other." She chewed the inside of her lip. "Not like you hurt me when you ordered me out of that room. Not like I hurt you when I didn't fight for you in Norway, and I walked away. I accept that I did that—but I'm *here* now. *You're here*. Let's...try?"

Charlie exhaled and rolled his chair back before standing. He gathered the wineglasses and gestured to the door. "Let's find someplace more comfortable, then."

She trailed after him, through the quiet penthouse to the opposite hall. They bypassed the kitchen, the dining room, the living room and even her bedroom. At the far end of the hall was a room she never went into—his bedroom.

He opened the door, and she hesitated. "Is that a good idea?"

"Trust me." Two very simple words, but a harder emotion to dredge up from the swampy morass of their mutual mistakes. He waited, though, and he didn't push. She licked her lips and nodded. She did trust him—if he wanted to sleep with her, well, hell, he could have had her on the table, in the foyer... Cutting off the lazy curl of desire that train of thought awoke, she stepped into his room.

Like hers, it had a large four-poster bed in the center of the nearly twice-the-size of her room, but it also had a little sitting area. Comfortable sofas arranged in an L shape with a pair of over-stuffed chairs. Video game controllers sat on the coffee table, across from a wide-screen television with a game system hooked up to it. A couple of blankets were tossed over the chairs and she picked out his favorite right away from the depression in the seat and the back.

"Welcome to my home away from home—no one will interrupt us here unless it's an emergency. The staff won't even ring through about dinner," Charlie explained, closing the door and turning the lock. "We have complete privacy. There are no cameras or surveillance in here either."

"Is there surveillance out there?" She pointed to the door, and her stomach dropped.

He nodded, carrying the wine and glasses over to the coffee table. He kicked off his shoes and the black loafers landed near the foot of the bed. "All royal residences are monitored twenty-four seven. I can—and have stipulated that they must shut it off when we're together. No one is watching when it is just the two of us."

She thought about her walk through the living room in the T-shirt, even if it covered the panties. "God." Sinking down on one of the sofas, she buried her face in her hands. "Okay, I'm more than a little humiliated at the moment."

Charlie laughed. He poured the wine. "You have fantastic legs and security are highly trained experts interested in keeping you safe, not ogling you. I promise."

Instead of sitting opposite her, he sat down on the corner of the second sofa closest to her. He held out a glass. "I accept your proposal."

Of course, now that he agreed and they were settled in a room behind locked doors, she didn't even know where to begin. They said nothing, the awkward silence stretching uncomfortably between them.

"I'm sorry I didn't tell you the truth about my title—or my family." He didn't wait for the question. The somber note in his voice arrested her heart. "I can make a thousand excuses—but I wanted you to like me for me and once you did, I worried that telling you the truth would change us. I didn't trust what we had, because I hadn't been honest from the beginning. Once I put it off, it became harder to tell you."

"But you told Richard." She bit the inside of her lip because it came out far more churlish than she intended. Yet she couldn't shake that hint of resentment. Charlie gave a piece of himself to his best friend—a piece he'd kept hidden from her.

"I did." He took a drink of the wine and stretched his legs out in front of him, but he didn't lower his gaze or try to avoid hers. "I told him because I wanted to tell you and I didn't know how. I needed his advice—but it's hard to tell someone what you think they should do if you don't have all the facts."

She tried to wrap her mind around that fact. "But you decided against telling me?"

"It sounds simple, but it's not." Charlie leaned forward and caught her hand. Stroking his thumb against her forefinger, he blew out a long breath. "I wanted to tell you—but I was torn. Did I want to tell you because you deserved to know? Or did I want to tell you because I wanted to shout to the world, look what I have with you? I went to an American university to get away from my family, from being an Andraste. I *liked* being Charlie. You and Richard are some of the only people I know that I am certain liked me for me— not for my title, not for my parents, not for my wealth or my position. You didn't want me for what I could do for you—" He laughed. "Actually, you didn't want me at all in the beginning. I had to compete with your studies and your jobs and your commitments to get you to even notice me and I loved that challenge."

"You were too damn good-looking," she muttered and swallowed two mouthfuls of wine in quick succession. Her idea or not, her nerves frayed. She wanted to be angry. She wanted to weep. She wanted to yell. She wanted to cheer. The conflict turned everything upside down.

"Yeah?" Charlie's grin grew. "How good-looking?"

"Sex-on-a-stick     good-looking." She'd promised honesty and as hot as her face grew with that admission, she planned to hold herself to it. "You with your sexy accent, modulated tones and cut body and your smile..." She glared at him. "Your smile turned me inside out and all I wanted to do was see it again—and ten years later, here I am turning into goo because you smile."

His grin grew. "I wish I were as eloquent—it was your breasts for me."

"My breasts?" Her jaw fell open. Did he really just say that?

"Yeah. You wore this little T-shirt with a V-neck and it dipped just low enough to reveal the edge of that dark beauty spot on your right breast. It—it was provocative. That you were sassy, dismissive and altogether focused on everything but me, that had its appeal too."

A shiver rippled over her skin and she couldn't stop staring at him. "So you told Richard and what did he say?"

"That you deserved to know the truth, but I better be damn sure. Because if my life was as I described it, involving you in it might not be what you wanted. I could tell you the truth and lose you in the same breath." His grin faded. "I thought about it all that summer, tried to start the conversation a million times in my head. But when we came back to campus that autumn, I was so damn happy to see you, I didn't want to spoil it."

She'd missed him that summer too. They'd talked every chance they got, but he was in Europe and she was home on the farm and their schedules conflicted more often than fell into sync.

"And once we moved in together...you really couldn't tell me." It wasn't a question. She understood, the longer he went without telling her, the messier it became. "But why did you make plans with me? For the future?"

"Because I wanted that future with you. Anna—if my father hadn't passed away, I wouldn't have been tied to the family business or to the royal business. I would have to make an appearance once or twice a year then I could have stayed away and been with you. I thought I would tell you after we graduated—when we took our first vacation together. I planned to whisk you away to this sunny little spot in the Mediterranean, hole up in an island paradise, confess all my sins and then make love to you until you forgave me and we worked something out."

Her heart squeezed at the description. He let go of her hand to refill their wineglasses. The half glass had already taken the edge of the jittery feeling inside her skin.

"But when my father passed so unexpectedly, my security had to get me home—they had to inform me—because my role changed." He didn't look at her. "But you couldn't forgive the deception, I think. You never said it to my face and I honestly was very distracted—" He blew out a hard breath. "But why did you leave that night? Why did you leave that *way*? Why didn't you *talk* to me?"

"I always thought it was because you lied."

The fires of the past singed her soul, but it was the right question to ask. "Because you didn't have *time* for me. You were gone. Tied up in meetings. You left. I waited for you to talk to me—to tell me all the things you just said." Licking the wine off her lips, she hunched her shoulders and shook her head slowly. "But I think that was my excuse—and far from my proudest moment."

A frown gathered between his eyes. "So why then?"

"I got scared. You didn't seem to see me anymore. Because I didn't know what I really wanted. I didn't—when I started questioning everything we shared, I realized I didn't have a lot of faith in it. I'd been waiting for the other shoe to drop—for us to grow up and move away. Everyone said college romances don't last and that first loves are first loves, because there's a second or a third." She cringed at how this must sound, but bald honesty cut through the political correctness of it all. "I couldn't stop thinking that if you didn't want me to know who you really were, what else didn't you want to share with me and what did I want? Did I even want to be a princess? Not that you ever asked."

"I think I understand. But why not talk to me? Why not come and tell me what you were feeling? Why didn't you trust me?"

"*You* didn't have time. You were always rushing somewhere else. I didn't even see you at night and because dammit, you're *that* guy." She rose and gave into the urge to pace. The wine took the edge off and loosened some of the tension in her muscles, but her brain and her gut remained in turmoil. "You're beautiful and amazing and the best guy and now you're a prince? I was there, Charlie—they were all bowing to you and Your Highnessing you and you were so calm. So utterly patient with every single person. You were with your mom, you were meeting with attorneys—you were focused and..."

He rose and caught her arm, turning her around so she had to look at him. "And what?"

"And you weren't Charlie. You were this Prince Andraste and they needed you. And I knew even if I told you all these crazy thoughts in my head, all these questions, you would address them in the same calm way you were taking with everyone else. Then I thought you would convince me to stay..." Tears burned in her eyes, her voice hitching around the lump in her throat. "I didn't know if that was what I wanted. So I left. I told myself it would be easier, simpler, and if you really wanted me...as something more than a college fling..." She coughed and swiped at one of the tears escaping to roll down her cheek.

"I would come after you." He wrapped his arms around her and pulled her close, she burrowed into the hug. God, she needed this.

"Yeah."

"I thought if you wanted me, you would come back," he murmured against her hair. "I didn't understand why you left. I thought you might need time so I tried to give it to you and then..." He sighed.

"Life went on without us." Pulling back, she rubbed her face and downed the rest of the wineglass. "Are we too stupid for a relationship or what?"

He chuckled softly and stroked her cheek. "No. We were young and foolish, not stupid. Why didn't you come back?"

"I didn't see a place for me there. You never —" She let go of that thought and rephrased it. Bluntness needed to be tempered by wisdom. "In all the times we talked about our future, you never asked me to marry you. We never discussed marriage. We never discussed what that... *future*...really meant. Why didn't you come after me?"

"Because I didn't think that was what you wanted. You left. You went back to the States, you moved out of our apartment—you closed the door. I wanted *you* to open it again." Anger edged his words. "I waited for a long time. I followed your career, I watched where you went and what you did...and there was so much to do—a steep learning curve for the family. My younger brothers needed me to provide stability, my mother leaned on me and when I finally got tired of waiting..."

He stopped, but he didn't bother to hide the tension locking up his jaw or the muscle ticking next to his eye.

"What?"

"You were engaged." The frosty tone cut through her. He pulled away before she could, draining his wineglass and refilling it. He added more to hers. "You were engaged to marry a fireman. Chad...something."

Her stomach sank.

"So, I assumed you moved on."

Resentment—and regret—stewed in her gut. "Then you started dating every gorgeous model you could get your hands on."

"Why not?" The flippant words, they weren't his and they didn't mute the anger and pain seething beneath. "You had a life. Why shouldn't I have mine?"

She couldn't fault him there. He paced around the coffee table. She walked over to the window. The physical distance mirroring the emotional hole in their relationship—the black pit threatening to chew them both up. "I didn't get married."

"Why is that?" He whirled to look at her. "Why didn't you marry him? This fireman—the local hero. I saw the photographs, he was much beloved. The kind of man who dedicated himself to helping others—it's what you always wanted..."

The vitriol underscoring his words lashed at her soul and found purchase, scoring little bloody wounds that bled inside.

"Or maybe you'd already met your police officer—that was a couple of years later, you were engaged to him. But you didn't marry then either. So who left whom? Did you end the engagement?" The air around him buzzed with judgment and jealousy.

She didn't drop her gaze or lower her eyes.

She wanted this—all the Band-Aids ripped off, all their injuries exposed. She just didn't expect the shame or the guilt gnawing at the jagged edges.

"I cared about them and when...and when they asked me to marry them, I said yes, because I thought it was what I wanted—what I was supposed to want. I thought, this is the life that I dreamed of. I finished my graduate studies in social work, I helped people—they helped people and I knew them. I knew what kind of men they were, I knew their devotion to their work, their dedication to their communities..."

"Yet you didn't marry them. Why, Anna? Why didn't you?" Charlie closed the gap and stood right in front of her, his dark eyes gleaming like lightning flashing in a black storm.

"Because they deserved better than me—they deserved better than a woman still in love with —" She couldn't finish it, but Charlie was relentless. He set aside their wineglasses and caught her face in his hands. His gaze searched hers.

"Who are you still in love with?" The silken demand delivered in a soft whisper.

"I'm in love with you, idiot. I never stopped loving you—"

His mouth crashed down on hers, primal, hot and filled with urgent need. She fisted her hands into his shirt, pulling him closer and surrendering to the dominant sweep of his tongue that invaded and took possession.

*I love you.*

# CHAPTER 13
## ARMAND

He couldn't get enough of her mouth. He devoured the sweet flavor of her, the wine lingering on her tongue, the hint of her shampoo teasing his nostrils and that inescapable flavor of *Anna*—the lushest, sweetest fruit in the world. Somewhere in his mind, the knowledge that they were supposed to be talking out their differences, baring their souls, ripping open their wounds—whatever she wanted to call it—poked at him.

*But she still loves me... Loves—not loved.* His heart raced. He didn't realize just how desperate to hear those three words he was until she hesitated. They flooded through him like water in the drought-starved land, filling in all the cracks that formed in her absence. He dragged his mouth away and drank in the sight of her.

He should let her go—put some distance between them and be reasonable and rational about everything.

The way she gazed at him erased those good

intentions. Her pupils were large and dilated. Her breath came in swift pants. Her breasts smashed against his chest, her leg thrust between his. Awareness hummed through him. Locking on to her gaze, he pushed all of his doubts aside.

"I want you." He picked her up and carried her over to the bed. He set her down gently, refusing to just toss her on the bed and fall on top of her no matter how long he'd wanted to do exactly that. He ran his fingers up and down her bare legs, savoring the silken texture of her skin. Her curls tousled around her face. The T-shirt rolled up at the waist, giving him a good view of the blue lace panties.

Sliding his knee onto the bed, he nudged the shirt upward, revealing the smooth plane of her belly. Blessed with generous curves, she was magnificent and the slope of her hip to her abdomen was a glorious thing. He dipped his head down to kiss the skin of her tummy just above the waistband of her panties and smiled. "Your skin is so soft."

Her fingers caressed his cheek and he looked up to see her staring at him, a private, sweet smile on her lips. Turning his head, he kissed her fingers once before continuing to push her—*his* —shirt up her body until the warm mounds of her breasts appeared. He let his gaze roam over her, stroking his hands up and down her sides, barely allowing himself the pleasure of cupping those sweet curves.

The feel of her—the taste of her—she was in his blood. He just wanted to enjoy the beauty of her. She began to move and he pushed her back into place, nudging the cotton up and over, helping her only long enough to pull the fabric free and toss it away.

The dark beauty spot on the curve of her right breast that so allured him stood out in stark relief against her creamy skin. "You still don't tan topless."

"Well, no..." She laughed and her skin went pink as a delightful blush suffused her. For all her sass and intelligence, she'd always possessed an inherent shyness—a modesty that was as attractive as it was charming.

She bumped her hips up at him, impatient, and her fingers plucked at his shirt, but Armand caught her hand and planted it on the bed. He stared at her sternly. "Behave."

"Behave?" Her eyebrows shot up and she narrowed her eyes.

"Yes." He leaned down and nipped her lower lip, drawing it between his in a hint of a teasing kiss. "You have to behave, because I want to play."

"But I want..."

He cupped her breast and flicked a finger over the nipple and she swallowed her words in a gasp.

"Behave." He repeated. "I've waited a long time for this present and I want to play. So you'll indulge me." It wasn't a question or a request. Her gaze sparked with rebellion, but her lips curved up and she relaxed her wrist under his hand. Nodding to himself, he went back to framing her sides, stroking the contour of her shape. He dreamed of this, the way they used to play—waking up to find her sprawled across the bed next to him. Teasing her awake with hot kisses.

So many wonderful memories... He leaned in and took one erect nipple into his mouth, sucking on it. The pebbled skin tightened under his tongue. He ran his hands up and down her body, hooking his thumbs into her panties until they scooted down her legs. He kissed a path between her nipples, showering both with kisses. Her hands flexed against the bed, clenching into fists and releasing. He released her nipple only long enough to pull the panties down and toss them away.

Sprawled on his bed was the most beautiful woman he ever knew—no top model in the world could compare with her lush curves or come-hither eyes—a siren who called to him across the world and the years.

He ached for her so bad, it hurt.

Stripping off his clothes, he joined her on the bed and pulled her into his arms. She flowed into them, fitting everywhere she was supposed to—softness to his hard, nails digging into his shoulders, her mouth open beneath his and devouring him in a kiss that was equal parts demand and surrender.

Their breath mingled and he lost track of everywhere her body touched his. The control he fought to hold on to slipped away. His imagination and desire were his worst enemies. Their hips rubbed together and his dick slid against the warm dampness of her cunt, her sudden moan matched his and he buried his face against her throat, licking and nipping little kisses to her ear. He drew on the lobe, sucking it as he tortured himself, rubbing the length of erection along the damp slickness of her entrance.

If he just positioned his hips...

"Condom," he murmured into her ear, tracing the whorls with his tongue.

"I don't care." She bit his shoulder and ran her foot up and down against the back of his leg. The action only served to grind his cock against her pussy. His eyes crossed in pleasure.

"It wasn't a request," he reminded her and cupped her breast, tweaking the nipple just hard enough to elicit another gasp. "Next to the bed, your side—condoms. Put one on me."

She let out a whimper of complaint and slid against him as she stretched out to open the drawer, she fumbled in it and came back with a foil package. He took advantage of the stretch to slide down and kiss her nipples again, massaging her breasts until she let out another long, low moan.

The foil package ripped and he smiled, sucking her nipple against his teeth and drumming it with this tongue before releasing her. He rolled onto his back and watched her beneath half-lowered eyelids. Pink and flush, her hands actually shook as she trailed a caress down to his cock. His dick twitched, as if eager for her touch, and he held his breath as her fingers shaped him, stroking up from base to tip.

He hissed out a breath between his teeth and her smile grew. He might be giving the orders, but she wasn't without power.

"Be careful," he warned. "I'm ready to come right now."

She bent and kissed the tip. His balls tightened up at the action, but so did the fist around his heart. It was a teasing kiss—she didn't swirl her tongue or try to suck on him. It was just the barest of caresses—her soft lips against the slit of his cock—a greeting, a lover's affection.

What little control he had left frayed. She rolled the condom on and he flipped her over, sliding between her thighs. He was wound tight, sweat dotted his arms and rolled down his chest. He settled his cock into place and stared into her eyes as he slid home. She stretched to accommodate him before she arched against the pillows. Her hair spilled out around her like some goddess receiving her due and damned if she wasn't one.

A ripple of pleasure raced out from his core as he pushed deeper—the slow penetration maddened him, but he didn't want to hurt her. His mind raced and his lungs burned, but finally he slid in to the hilt. She sighed and he closed his eyes, savoring the moment. Her arms wound around his neck and her mouth found his. They began to move together, rocking in a motion so familiar and heart wrenching that it shook him to his core.

She kissed him, tongue dueling with his, but

it was so Anna—as much giving as taking—and then it was her turn to suck and bite at his skin as she trailed kisses down his throat. He focused on holding the rhythm, driving her to her pleasure—she had to come and come soon or he would fly apart at the seams.

Her fingers dug into his ass, driving him deeper, and her whispery sighs turned to little cries as he ground against her with each stroke. He slid a hand between them, forcing his own eyes open to watch as he stroked two fingers against her clit. Her whole body arched as though electricity shot through her. She clamped down around his cock and cried out. He shook from the unrelenting pleasure pounding through him so fiercely it was almost painful. He drove harder, thrusting until the world faded to the motion of her body wrapped around him, and when she cried out a second time, he pitched over the edge with her.

Collapsing against her, he held her tight. Face buried against her throat, he couldn't think beyond the sensations rippling down his spine. It went beyond physical intimacy—he'd never been this connected to another person. Her heart raced, matching his beat for beat, where her breasts rubbed his chest.

"I love you," she whispered against him and he squeezed her close.

He loved her too.

*How the hell am I ever going to keep her safe?*

~

## ANNA

She closed her eyes, but didn't intend for sleep—
just a lazy drift on the pleasure still quaking in
her bones. They used to do this too—make love
and then lie there together for hours, sometimes
talking, sometimes saying nothing at all. They
didn't always need words to fill in those empty
spaces. Being together was enough. Charlie's
breath was alternately cool and hot against her
flushed skin. Every nerve hummed. When he insisted on caressing her sides earlier, she didn't
think he could possibly be aware of just how sensitive she was to each touch.

She missed this. *I missed him.*

"I need to get off you." His voice, muffled
against her throat, skimmed the surface of her
pleasure and doused it with a cold, hard reality.

He didn't sound pleased.

"You're fine."

While he squashed her to the bed, she didn't
care. She liked the feeling of his weight over her,
touching her, holding her. It made being together
again real, but he rolled away as if she hadn't
spoken. He made it to the edge of the bed and sat,
his back to her.

"Charlie?"

He glanced over his shoulder, but his unread-
able expression seemed a far cry from the tender
passion consuming them just minutes ago. "I just
need a moment, I'm going to wash up." He disappeared into the bathroom and she went cold.
Frost seemed to turn the room from a haze of hot

pleasure to frozen tundra. She reached for the T-shirt and pulled it on slowly. It took her longer to find her panties.

When he still hadn't emerged from the bathroom, the last lingering dregs of pleasure dried up. Uneasy, she paced a step toward the bathroom and then away. Looking back, she found him standing in the doorway, a brooding look on his face.

"My apologies, Anna." His voice—so cultured, so well mannered, so civilized—betrayed none of the husky tones he used when he issued orders just a little while before.

"For what?" She floundered, like someone had tossed her into the deep end of the pool and forgot to mention it had no bottom.

"For...for making love—we were not ready for that and we shouldn't have." Absolute calm dominated his voice—calm and distance. He'd dragged on a pair of pants while he was in the bathroom. Shirtless with the top button undone on his slacks, he looked rakish. But his expression wasn't that of sexy fun or teasing. "I overstepped myself."

"You're apologizing to me?" She couldn't quite believe her ears or her heart. Tension surged through her muscles and her right eye twitched.

"We came in here to talk and clear the air."

"I think we cleared up a lot—" *And I said I love you.* But the last she held back, she didn't even mean to hold it back, but...

*You didn't say you love me.*

Her legs went rubbery and she sat abruptly on the edge of the bed. Her eyes burned, but she blinked them furiously, refusing to give in to tears. She didn't look at Charlie, but he walked across the room to the sitting area. He picked up one of the wineglasses and drained the contents.

Controlling the urge to scream, she looked up to find him standing in front of her, wineglass in hand. She took it and sniffed once. "I wish you wouldn't apologize for it. I thought..." *What had I thought? That we'd have sex and it would all be better?*

"Yes, I know." He sat next to her, close enough to feel, but not quite touching. "And that is why I'm apologizing..."

*God, no, you will not talk to me in that...that... prince voice. Not again.* She surged to her feet, ignoring the wine she sloshed, and strode toward the door.

"So much for not running. We have hours left on your deal." His voice, razor sharp, cut her stumbling steps to a halt. "Isn't that what you said? All will be forgiven—no matter what we say or how angry we become?"

Pivoting slowly, she looked back. He stood at the edge of the bed, his hands in his pockets, his jaw tight and his eyes narrowed. He walked toward her, slowly, almost stalking.

"That is what you said? We'll rip the Band-Aid off?" His voice was lazy silk and steel twined together. It stroked her and cut her in the same breath. "We won't dance around our mistakes— ask any question, get any answer..."

She backed into the door. He didn't slow until he stood right in front of her. "You keep running, Anna."

"I know." She winced, and as much as she wanted to look away, she couldn't. He seemed to draw all the light in the room—it shone against his black hair and rippled over the gleam of sweat on his skin.

"Do you? I buried my father and I needed you. You were there one moment and gone the next." His nostrils flared. She thought she'd known what angry was like, but he was furious. With her or with himself—she wasn't sure.

"I was stupid, Charlie. I was...foolish and naïve and a whole lot of other words. I can't apologize enough for the choice. It cost me—it cost you."

"It cost *us*." He took a step back. "I blamed myself for it. I took issue with keeping the truth from you. You left—because you found out the truth, not because of the lie." He stretched his hands out. "And this is the truth. In this room, I am Charlie. I am free of the encumbrances of my title. I can be me. Out there? I am the Prince Armand, Grand Duke Andraste—and five thousand employees, servants, staff and family depend on me to keep my head. To see to their welfare. I don't have a country. I have a company. I have a family. This is my life, Anna. The bald truth of it."

He stalked away to stand before the windows. The sunset in the distance and the illumination of it seemed surreal. They hadn't been in that room long enough for the day to even end and yet—

It seemed centuries.

Heart thundering in her ears, she wavered on the precipice. As melodramatic as it seemed, she knew their future waited on her decision.

"I'm only sorry we made love because I cannot offer you anything more now than I could then. I am a prince without a nation, a grand duke with responsibilities, and they will not go away with our reunion. I will never be that boy in college who shared an apartment and made do with a hodgepodge of furniture and a miniscule budget—enjoying water instead of wine because it was cheaper. I'm still the man you left before."

Beneath the churning surface of his fury and ice echoed a sad wistfulness. Setting her wineglass on the coffee table, she walked over, wrapped her arms around his middle and leaned her head against his back. His skin seemed hot and cold. His rigid muscles loosened the longer she stood there, just holding him. He finally settled a hand atop hers on his belly.

"I'm not sorry," she murmured against his back. "I'm not sorry we made love—I can't be. It was like being where I belonged and I won't regret it—even if you decide I'm not worth the trouble."

He sighed. "You wouldn't even be here if I hadn't demanded you come see me."

"I'm here because I want to be here." *Doesn't he love me just the least little bit?*

"Anna—"

"No. You don't have to say anything or mean anything or even promise anything." She couldn't believe the words coming out of her mouth, but she meant them. She loved him enough for both right now—if it took her the rest of her life to earn his forgiveness, well, then that was what she would do. "I'm here. You're here. We can talk—we can make love—we can play video games."

The lightness in the last fell flat, but he turned in her arms and wrapped her in his embrace. He tucked his chin against her head and she hid there, the illusion of safety better than any rejection. "It's not fair to you..." he began.

"I don't care. I just told you I'm not leaving." *Not again.*

He sighed and kissed her forehead. "Then let me at least send for supper." He pulled free of her arms and walked over to the phone. This—a good portion of this—was her fault.

She wouldn't let the prince push her away—not when she'd run from Charlie because of the prince before. They could fix this. She didn't know how, but they had to be able to fix it. They'd just found each other again.

# CHAPTER 14
# ARMAND

He flipped through the newspaper, barely reading any of the words. Waking with Anna in his arms was the sweetest ache he'd ever experienced. Slipping out of the bed while she still slept, he'd showered, dressed and settled himself in the dining room. They'd talked for hours, not that he recalled much of the conversation after setting her on the bed and—

He cut off the line of thought.

His body hummed to awareness, seemingly experiencing no conflict between physical desire and the right thing to do.

The door opened down the hall and he kept his gaze focused on the newspaper. Taking advantage of her vulnerability, assuming a future they didn't have—these were not the best choices he could have made. Hell, of late, he only seemed to make foolish, impulsive decisions—decisions that left her open to danger. The crosshair-framed snapshots of her scrolled through his mind when her sweet scent wrapped around him. She poured herself coffee and joined him at the table, but instead of taking a seat at the end, she pulled out the chair next to his.

"Good morning," she murmured in a voice still husky from sleep. The low, throaty whisper went right to his groin.

"Morning." He glanced at her over the paper once. The image of her seared itself to his brain. Damp curls, freshly showered and rosy cheeks because she liked her water boiling. She wore a thin sweater top in the deepest shade of blue—a perfect contrast for her skin.

"You can't ignore me forever," she murmured, taking a sip of her coffee.

He kept his gaze affixed to the business column in front of him. "I'm not ignoring you."

"Charlie—"

"However." He folded the paper shut abruptly. Calling him Charlie provoked a longing for what they could never have and he'd been an idiot—a foolish, irresponsible idiot to think otherwise. Unlike George and Sebastian, he did not have even the illusion of freedom to indulge in a "normal" life. "I have meetings today that can't be avoided, so it may be late before I return."

"I thought you took time off to work with me on the fund."

"Unfortunately, clearing my schedule is not a simple prospect. Emergencies come up. You will be working on the fourteenth today?" He rose, his coffee not even half-finished.

"Sure." The single-syllable response wasn't

like her. He pushed the chair in and turned to find her standing in front of him. Blocking his path.

"Yes?"

She planted a hand against his chest and his heart shuddered. Up on her tiptoes she came and her lips brushed his mouth. With a low groan, he slid his arms around her and returned the kiss, deepening it until she melted in his arms. The sweet taste of her toothpaste added a crisp bite to the hint of coffee. Her arms glided around his neck and she opened to the invasion of his tongue. Sweet. Soft. Perfect.

It took every ounce of willpower he possessed to let her go. Her kiss lingering on his lips, he couldn't ignore the drowsy desire in her half-lidded eyes. While he couldn't ignore it, he also couldn't afford to take advantage of her again. Anna's time with him was limited—they would solve the issue of the death threats and she would be free to go. Safer—far, far away from him.

He had no intentions of letting her life end. It would destroy him to lose her. It would end him to mourn her.

"I'll see you later?" She straightened his tie, adjusting the knot and smoothing the silk down.

"Don't wait up for me, I might be very late." Time to go. Releasing her took effort and he spared her a quick smile. Five steps to the door and he was out. He punched the elevator button and stepped inside. She didn't follow him— thankfully. The elevator paused on the next floor and his security chief stood there.

"You're going out today, Your Highness?"

Of course, he failed to notify security of his rather abrupt change in plans.

"Yes, I have some appointments that must be kept. We'll start with the FBI field office and get a report on their investigation." He was certain the FBI wouldn't be enthusiastic about the visit, but it was the first thing to come to mind—after those photos, he didn't want anyone forgetting the threat to Anna.

"Very well, Your Highness." Peterson motioned to two men behind him and they stepped into the elevator. "I'll call down for the car. If you wouldn't mind giving the driver your full itinerary, we'll do our best to accommodate it." The man didn't quite chastise him, but he also didn't bother to veil the disapproval in his voice.

His security, circumspect as always, made no comment on the descent to the garage. A black SUV and two sedans awaited his arrival. In addition to the two men riding down with him, six more waited on the ground floor.

Peterson wasn't taking any chances with his charges. His thoroughness and attention to detail were two of the main reasons he earned his position as head of the family's security. In the backseat, Armand pulled out his phone and sent a text to Richard. In minutes, he arranged a game of racquetball.

He needed to slam something around.

"Destinations, sir?"

"FBI field office, and then we'll meet Mr. Prentiss at the club."

The driver was silent, but Armand knew the

information would be communicated to Peterson. "Yes, sir. Mr. Peterson is sending a car ahead to the club." He slid his sunglasses on and the cars rolled out.

At the FBI field office, Armand stood in a lounge that had definitely seen better days. The agents weren't prepared for his arrival, but the office's senior agent in charge arranged for coffee and walked in with a file in one hand and the other outstretched for a firm handshake.

"We've eliminated another four suspects and we think we have another lead that may interest you." The man began without preamble and gestured for Armand to take a seat. Americans rarely stood on ceremony and while some seemed to worry that would upset him, he actually enjoyed the normal treatment.

The sofa was hard, lumpy and desperately unforgiving. He chose to sit on the edge. The agent flipped open a file and turned it around to show him a picture. The first thing that struck him were the dead eyes. The second were the tattoos. The symbols inscribed to the man's neck and arms came directly from prison.

A Russian prison.

"His name is Yuri Markov, he's a Russian citizen and we believe he entered the United States illegally about six months ago." Six months—was that before or after George was in Belaria? Did it matter? His timing couldn't have been a coincidence, he'd arrived...

Just in time for a princess's wedding.

"Now, Markov—he's a foot soldier. His sheet

is one long list of larceny, assault, battery and three attempted murder charges and four alleged murders, but he was never prosecuted on those. The interesting part is that Markov has ties to the Kachusov family in Belaria. He handles some business for them, but he's a foot soldier."

*Belaria.* Ice dripped down his spine.

"I see you are familiar with the country."

Armand nodded once. "Yes. It has been in dire straits in the last few years, but shale leases in the mountains may provide a key to turning their economy around if they do not destroy the environment first." A number of companies competed for the leases—leases held by the Kachusov family. Zuran Kachusov served as Belaria's first president and his sons were all generals in the tiny country's military—but beyond that, they were suspected of multiple ties to bratva families in St. Petersburg.

"The threats are coming from the Kachusovs?" Cool and impersonal—it was the only way to handle the rage building inside.

"We can't say that for sure, sir. What we can tell you is that as of three days ago, Yuri received three payments totaling half a million dollars and three photographs."

Amazing how the FBI seemed to know all this. Did they have Markov in custody?

"Unfortunately, Markov seemed aware of the surveillance and gave us the slip. We believe that the money represents deposits or payoffs for targets. Currently, we have several to choose from here in the city—your cousin, her husband, yourself and your brothers."

"And Miss Novak." Armand did not want the FBI to ignore the credible threat to her.

"Yes, sir—Miss Novak is considered a lower risk because while we have threats targeting her, we believe it's a decoy designed to stretch your resources thin."

"I appreciate your candor, Agent. However, Miss Novak has been targeted because of her association with me—so you will not lower her 'risk.' My cousin and her husband are leaving on a long-overdue second honeymoon this afternoon." He would speak to Daniel about it. The software programmer could work anywhere and his company was on solid footing. He could afford to take Alyx away to the islands—such as the isolated one the Andraste family owned. It wouldn't take long to make the arrangements.

"As for my brothers, George will return to Europe within a day or two. He can stay at the family compound in Norway, it has as much security as here, if not more. Sebastian can return to the Mediterranean." While Norway was closer to Belaria, it was farther than the current threat.

"Prince Armand, you'll forgive me, but I do have a couple of questions for your youngest brother before he leaves." The statement caught Armand off guard. He wasn't sure he could convince Anna to take a long vacation—perhaps in Australia, halfway around the world from these issues.

"Why do you need to question George?" No

one was touching his brother, not even the federal authorities.

The older man looked uneasy, his mouth compressed, his jaw tightened, and he smoothed his tie—a nervous habit he repeated twice since Armand had sat down. "Were you aware of Prince George's visit to Belaria last year?"

Armand knew his brother's itineraries. They were always filed with his office, Gretchen kept updates in the calendar so he knew what country and time zones his brothers were in. "This is related to his work with the Pulshkyn Party?" For all of George's jet-setting ways, he did occasionally become passionate about a cause. The Pulshkyn Party in Belaria was a small political movement seeking to preserve Belaria's cultural and environmental heritage—and stop foreign companies from plundering them.

"Washington thinks so." The agent flipped the file to another page. "During his time in Belaria, the prince attended a dozen rallies, thirty-two coffee meetings, and donated in excess of one million dollars to the Pulshkyn Party's movement. He was photographed with Bogdan Zhabin, the head of that movement."

George's growing notoriety in the region was the primary reason Armand ordered him to leave Belaria. They couldn't afford the press coverage or the backlash—particularly the two bombings of Andraste factories on the border.

"Sir, in the last six months, the Pulshkyn platform and rallying cry has become a return to their roots—to their monarchy. They want to put you back on a throne."

Rumors had filtered through the reports about that wrinkle—rumors Peterson confirmed the day before. Armand had instructed his executives and agents to play it down—particularly since he had no intentions of accepting a throne his great-grandfather was deposed from. "Yes, I am aware. These movements crop up from time to time in the destabilized areas of the former Soviet Union. It will pass."

"That's the rub, sir. Our analysts don't see it passing anytime soon. At nearly every appearance of the Kachusov family in the last six weeks, Pulshkyn supporters have picketed and staged demonstrations—and the banner they are using features you." As if he'd been waiting for this moment, the agent gestured to the television and a series of images played out. The demonstrations seemed to begin peaceful, but always ended in violence. Armand's face plastered to banners. The Russian placards read "Long Live Andraste," "Bring the Andraste Home," and even more disturbingly, "Belaria Needs Her Czar."

"Then the threats are directly related to this." It didn't take a genius to put it together. It also explained the threat to Anna. A bachelor grand duke offered an ideal—a royal couple could be a dream, particularly if it promised issue and security for the royal line. He should never have forced that meeting with her. If not for his own need to see her again, she would be safe. "Would you please make sure my security director Peterson receives a copy of this—particularly the photograph of Markov?"

"Of course. Sir, if you don't mind the suggestion—I think you should keep a lower profile for a bit, perhaps take a vacation of your own far away from the limelight—"

Armand rose and shook the agent's hand. "Thank you for your concern. We have dealt with threats like this before and no doubt will again."

No, if anything, he needed to raise his profile. Draw the attention to himself—take the spotlights off Anna, George, and Sebastian. So far none of the threats seemed aimed at his mother, but he would increase her security nonetheless. The agent offered to walk him out—however, Armand's security detail was large enough they'd parked in the subbasement beneath the FBI's office.

In the car, he made a few phone calls—including one to verify Anna was still safely tucked away in the Petersburg Tower.

"Country club, sir?"

"Yes. Call Mr. Prentiss and let him know we will meet him there." Armand dialed his secretary. "Gretchen, good morning. Would you put a phone call in to Nikole's agent, Valeria's, and Zoey's as well. I would like all three in attendance next week. Yes, I received the memo that our launch had been delayed. Take care of any expenses with flying the ladies in—they can stay in our suites at the Beverly Wilshire. Very good."

He rang off and stared at his phone. Anna's number was the third on the list. She wouldn't care for the changes to the scholarship fund launch, but the renovations at the concert hall and security concerns required a few extra days.

Time enough for him to remove her as a target.

～

RICHARD CAUGHT the ball on the rebound and sent it slamming toward the wall. Armand pivoted and nailed it with a backswing. They played silently, only the sound of the ball thwacking off their rackets or rebounding off the wall filling the court. He shut off all the distractions—the security standing around the court, placed in obvious positions with their black-suited backs to him. He closed down the niggling desire to call his security to check on Anna, or better still, call Anna himself.

He shut it all off. Sweat soaked through his shirt and stung at his eyes. His lungs burned as he twisted, turned and caught every volley Richard lobbed. But it all halted when Richard missed his swing and the ball bounced off the safety glass behind him.

"Two-one." Richard tucked his racket under an arm and walked over to claim the water bottles from the wall holder. He tossed one to Armand underhanded and unscrewed the other to drink. "So, how did it go last night?"

Armand took his time draining the bottle. "It was fine. Another game?"

The attorney stared at him. "Fine? You stalk

the woman? You talked about her for years and then conspicuously avoided any mention of her for longer? Then you demand she meets with you and move her into the penthouse? And it was *fine?*"

Bouncing the ball once, Armand pointedly took aim and sent the ball at the wall. Richard barely caught it and drove it back. "What's up?"

"Nothing. Playing." He smacked it hard and sent it up and flinging back. Richard jerked hard to the left and smacked it on the rebound.

"That woman had more on her mind than just talking—what happened?" Like a bulldog with a bone, Richard wouldn't let it go.

"We talked about her leaving." Armand nearly missed and his hamstring burned as he overcompensated. Flexing his toes inside the shoe, he and Richard danced side to side, slicing, cutting and backhanding the ball. Every hard slap of the ball to his racket loosened the landslide of tension sitting on his chest.

"Couldn't have been easy."

"It wasn't." He'd thought it would be—hashing it out, hearing it from her exactly why she left him all those years ago. But that scar turned out to be hiding a bloody, festering wound. He wanted to strangle her. He wanted to kiss her. He wanted to keep her close, make up for all that lost time, and he never wanted to see her again—because if she wasn't with him, she wasn't in danger.

The conflict oozed through him like a cancer,

eating away at his good judgment and common sense.

However, Richard didn't seem satisfied. "And?"

"And nothing." Armand's turn to miss the ball, he swore and paced around in a circle trying to catch his breath.

"Yeah, I see your nothing and call bullshit. What happened?" Richard picked up the ball and held it hostage while he took another drink.

"It's not important." He dismissed the whole matter with a wave of his hand.

Richard snorted. "You know, I can stand in front of the press all day and spin the 'they're just good friends' line all you want—in fact I just did. But you're not fooling me."

"Let's play." He didn't want to discuss it, not even with Richard.

"Yeah, okay—we can play when you stop playing aloof prince." His oldest friend bounced the ball once, then twice, but didn't serve. "Talk to me."

"It doesn't matter, Richard. In a few days, we'll have the situation sorted out and she will go back to her life and I will go back to mine." Perhaps a ski trip—or a cabin on top of an icy remote mountain—as far from sunshine, California and Anna as he could. It would take some time to get her out of his system again, but he'd managed it once.

"Man, what are you doing?" Richard rarely fell back on slang unless he was genuinely concerned.

"I am fixing what I shouldn't have broken." Armand eased the pressure on his hamstring and stretched.

"So, what happened? She tell you no?"

"No." Armand shook his head and walked over to claim another bottle of water. "She said she loved me."

"That's great." Richard patted him on the back but halted when Armand gave him a baleful look. "Well, isn't it?"

"No. Anna isn't cut out for this life—for the responsibilities and requirements. She certainly doesn't need to be in the line of fire. Like I said, in a few days, we'll have it sorted out and we can all go back to our lives." He snatched the ball out of Richard's hand and set the water bottle down. "That will be the end of that chapter."

"You love her." Richard's words cut through Armand and he missed his serve.

"Damn it." He blew out a breath.

"Yeah, you definitely love her. You don't curse. You never miss a serve." Richard caught the ball and bounced it against the ground, catching it. "So...what happened?"

"I love her more than my own life, but I don't trust her." He stared at his best friend. "She has one foot out the door. She hasn't wanted to be here from the beginning—and if I hadn't been an ass, she wouldn't still be there now. And she needs to be out the door. It's *safer* for her."

"Maybe she wasn't thrilled about seeing you again in the beginning—but I saw how she looked at you last night. I remember that look.

Don't let this go because you don't think you deserve—"

"Enough, Richard. It's done. I should have realized that she made the right choice all those years ago and buried it then. I will not be a fool twice."

"That's the prince talking. Where's my friend? You know, the guy who gets drunk once a year and reminisces about her?"

"He's sober and the truth is not as attractive as the fantasy. That's all she can ever be." The ache in his soul ballooned open. He wanted to trust her words; he wanted to believe that they could make it work this time—a clean, fresh start —but this wasn't a fresh start or a particularly clean one. Old wounds infected them both and new challenges were always waiting on the horizon. He'd put her in harm's way, close quarters and familiarity did the rest. As soon as her life went back to normal, he wouldn't have a place in it. As it should be.

"You're an idiot." Richard served and they went back to the game. Thirty minutes later, Armand buttoned his shirt in the private locker room. His security always arranged for one. Richard's membership meant he could use any he pleased, but he left Armand alone until after the shower.

"I'm going to say this to you once." Richard sat on the edge of a bench and tied his dress shoes. He would return to his office, while Armand had to go back to the tower.

To Anna.

"Really? I thought we'd discussed it a few times already." The prince spared him a look in the mirror before looping the tie around his neck.

"I talked, you didn't listen. A man in love isn't usually the most reasonable of people." Richard stood and reached for his own tie. "You less than most, but you forget, my friend, I was there when she left. You kept it together for everyone, you leaned on your duty and your honor so hard. I thought you were going to forget how to be a person. She hurt you. She's a bitch—"

"Watch your tone." Armand's gaze narrowed.

"Why? She's just going to leave. Why does she deserve any kind of special treatment? Granted, she has a sweet ass but if the bitch couldn't handle—"

Armand's fist flew and connected with Richard's jaw. The impact burned through his arm and his knuckles caught on fire. The attorney stumbled back two feet and bounced against the front of a locker.

Shaking his hand, Armand continued to glare. "You don't look at her ass and you don't call her names."

Richard laughed and rubbed his face. "Thank you for making my point for me."

"You're an asshole." Damn Richard for playing him—but he'd always known exactly what buttons to push and when to call Armand on his bullshit. It didn't make the pill of truth any easier to swallow.

"I'm paid to be an asshole, but for you? No charge." Stretching his jaw, he winced. "Look, you tell yourself whatever you need to in order to sleep at night. But you haven't looked at a woman the way you look at her since she left. You haven't done crazy, impulsive shit without her either. You have a chance to make it work now. She knows who you are—she knows what you are. Go for it. If she leaves, she leaves. But don't make that the easy choice because you're afraid." Grabbing his jacket and slinging it on, Richard sighed. "Look, I have to be in court this afternoon. I'll call you later, swing by for a drink. But think about it. You wanted this chance—you have it. Don't piss it away because of fear."

"Rick." Armand stopped him at the door. "Thanks. And sorry about hitting you."

"You're welcome, and no, you're not." He grinned.

"No. No, I'm really not." The hollow laugh felt good and he sat on the bench Richard abandoned. Alone, he stared at the three swelling knuckles on his right hand.

His phone rang in his pocket and he pulled it out. Anna's face flashed up on the screen and he stared at it for a long moment. They needed to talk—but not over the phone. He declined the call and rose. After stuffing the phone back into his pocket, he finished his tie and pulled on his own suit jacket. He had to look the part before he walked out the door.

If she was destined to leave him, it shouldn't bother him to break her heart first. Richard's words echoed in his ears. *Thanks for proving my point. You love her. So why not go for it?*

Loving her could destroy her—she could heal from a broken heart.

They were living proof of that.

~

HE STOPPED at Daniel's office on his way back to the tower. His cousin-in-law was already hustling it back to Beverly Hills. The thirty-minute conversation and two phone calls later, and the couple were already on their way out of town. He slid into the SUV and the driver's cell rang. Armand's rang at the same time and several of his security detail closed in around the car.

Pulling the phone out, he saw Peterson's number. "What's wrong?" The sedans moved in closer, and the detail ranged out, with a man at each door to the SUV.

"Your Highness, there's been an accident."

"Anna?" His chest compressed.

"No, sir. Mr. Prentiss. About fifteen minutes ago, on the 5."

*Richard?*

"Your Highness, you need to return to the tower... I'm instructing security—"

"No, I need to go to the hospital." Armand glanced at the driver. "Find out where they took him and get us there now."

"Yes, sir."

"Sir, I have to insist—" Peterson rarely took that tone with him, the man didn't give him orders.

"I said no. I'm going to the hospital. Send

more men over if you have to, and get me a status on his condition—"

The security chief cut him off. "Mr. Prentiss was run off the road. LAPD on scene have already confirmed multiple hits to his car, it went down an embankment and rolled. I really need you back at the tower."

"As soon as I see him." He hung up on Peterson. "Go." He snapped at the driver. One of the guards slipped into the passenger seat and the others raced to the sedans.

"He's on his way to County General," the guard said over his shoulder. "They airlifted him. We can be there in twenty minutes." Tires squealed as the SUV lurched into motion.

Ice rippled through Armand's veins. He protected everyone...

Everyone except his best friend.

# CHAPTER 15
## ANNA

Anna didn't even close the door to the apartment. She punched the elevator button and punched it again. And again. Her finger tapped the down button repeatedly until the doors dinged and it opened. Inside, she slipped her purse strap over her shoulder and hit the lobby button. Her insides were knotted so tight she could feel the tension snapping in her muscles. She hit the lobby button again. "C'mon."

The elevator halted three floors below and she bit back a scream as the doors opened. Kyle Johnson stood there, his expression fierce. "Miss Novak. You don't have any trips planned today."

"No. But my friend—Charlie's friend—Richard Prentiss was in a car accident. Charlie's going to the hospital, I need to be there for him."

Kyle shook his head slowly. "Ma'am, that's not the best idea. We're already stretched thin with the prince's presence at the hospital and securing Mr. Prentiss and the scene—"

"You don't understand. Richard is Charlie's best friend in the entire world. I'm going to that hospital and you can go with me and I'll do exactly what you say to stay safe or you can get the hell out of my way. But if you plan to make me stay here, kidnapping is against the law..." Her voice cracked at the end of the sentence. She couldn't believe Richard had been hurt. Charlie couldn't be taking it well—and no matter how cool and remote he was that morning, this was his best friend.

She had to be there.

The security guard held up a hand. "Okay, okay. Breathe." He pulled out his cell phone and stepped into the elevator. "This is Johnson. I need three unmarked and call in Fisher and Williams. Yes, Miss Novak is joining His Highness at County General." Inside the elevator, Kyle inserted a key and typed in a code. The doors slid shut.

Anna couldn't stand still, her right foot tapped impatiently.

"The press already know about the accident, but they don't have any details. They know His Highness is at the hospital, which means whoever caused the accident may as well. The FBI is on scene, as are LAPD. It could take us a little finessing to get in the door. Stay at my side, and keep your head down until I deliver you. No arguments, if it's not safe, we're leaving, understood?"

Her stomach twisted with nausea. "I understand, thank you."

"You're welcome. Mr. Prentiss is a good guy. He didn't deserve this."

The elevator doors opened to the garage. Like the day Kyle arrived to rescue her from the house, an SUV waited between two sedans. Two men in each sedan and a driver in the SUV. The garage security officer held the door open and Kyle held her elbow as she slipped inside. They closed the door and Kyle spoke to the other guard before he climbed in.

"Let's go." Kyle ordered the driver and gave her a reassuring nod.

The forty-five-minute drive from the tower was nightmarishly long. She sat on the edge of her seat, wearing a sore into the inside of her lip from chewing it. Kyle checked with the detail at the hospital twice—Richard was in surgery and they had nothing new to report.

Flashing blue-and-red lights on the top of three black-and-whites and tape kept the press back from the emergency entrance. The cars pulled right up to the ER and Kyle glanced back at her. "Stay."

He stepped out first, his eyes hidden behind dark shades. He scanned the area and glanced at the two men exiting the building, dressed identically to him—they seemed to know each other.

He opened her door and the flashbulbs went off and questions were shouted. She did exactly what Kyle told her to do, walking right next to him, shielded on all sides. The three men stayed with her to the elevator and they rode up in silence.

On the surgical floor, the doors opened. Two black-suited security guards stood there, along with an LAPD officer. Kyle still stepped out first and she waited for his hand to extend, motioning her to exit before following. He led her down the sterile hallway with its cream-colored walls. It reeked of antiseptic and industrial cleaners. Only medical staff moved about the quiet floor in their green scrubs—and more black-suited security.

She lost count at fifteen.

Her insides trembled as they arrived at a closed door. The guard in front of it opened the door and everything else around her faded away. Charlie stood in the center of the room, his hands in his pockets, his suit jacket gone, a haggard and lonely look frozen on his beautiful face. She dropped her purse in the chair and ran toward him.

He turned as she cleared the door and then she was there, wrapping her arms around him. He remained perfectly still, then he enfolded her, squeezing tight. She closed her eyes and just held on to him. A shudder seemed to ripple through him and he gathered her closer, his face buried against her hair. She didn't know what to say— what could she possibly say? She held him tighter, just being with him—being there for him.

They stood that way for minutes, or maybe it was hours—she didn't know and she didn't care. The door opened again. Charlie lifted his head, but he didn't let her go. "Your Highness, Mr. Prentiss is doing well in the surgery. We had some internal bleeding and we've managed to stop most of it. He listed you as having medical power of attorney and I need to discuss the situation with his spleen."

Charlie cleared his throat. "Go on."

The doctor cut a look toward her but focused the majority of her attention on Charlie. "The trauma of the accident has left Mr. Prentiss with a lacerated spleen. We're having trouble stopping the bleeding, we can remove it or we can continue the efforts to halt the bleed and let him recover. But he also has trauma to one of his kidneys and three broken ribs—and we had to reinflate one lung." The doctor gave them a reassuring smile. "This all sounds very bad, but the majority of the trauma is localized on the organs —our primary task is to stanch the bleeds."

"And you need my permission to remove the spleen if you can't?" Charlie's attention was laser sharp on the surgeon, but worry darkened every syllable.

"The spleen and one kidney. He can survive with one kidney and live a relatively normal life. He'll need immunizations for the spleen."

"Do whatever is medically necessary to save his life. If you need specialists, name them and I'll get them here." Charlie's voice was hard, unyielding and blunt.

"I appreciate that, Your Highness. I assure you that Doctor Nelson and Doctor Woodard are the best general surgeons in the state." The doctor gave him a comforting smile. "I'll be out to let you know as soon as they are done."

Charlie said nothing as the doctor left. Anna rubbed her hands against his back, a slow, circular massage. He sighed. "You should be at the tower." But he made no move to release her.

"I am right where I should be," she murmured against his chest.

"It's not safe. Anna, the accident—it wasn't an accident." His accent grew more pronounced and his voice huskier, laced with tears and self-recrimination. He blamed himself.

"Shh. I know. Kyle made sure it was clear to bring me in and I stayed right with him all the way to this door." The tiny surgical waiting room offered no windows and only one door—and that was guarded by a half a dozen of the prince's security.

"I need to call his family."

"I can do that." She leaned back, lifting her chin and studying his face.

Agony writhed in his dark eyes. "I don't have much to tell them."

"It's enough to let them know what's going on. Is his sister still in London?" Barbara Prentiss was an actress in musical theater.

"Yes. His mother and stepfather are on a cruise."

"Okay, so it's—" She looked at the clock on the wall and did the mental math. "After midnight in London. We can wait until after surgery to wake her."

Charlie nodded jerkily. A muscle ticked in his face. "That might be best."

"Let's sit down, okay? Can I get you some coffee? Anything?"

He let her guide him over to an uncomfortable-looking sofa, but held on to her hand and tugged her to sit down when she would have gone to get him a drink. He sandwiched her hand between his and she pressed her head against his shoulder.

"I played racquetball with him today." He stared at the floor, but she didn't think he saw anything. "He had meetings and I made him cancel them because I needed a game. If I hadn't..."

"Don't do that, Charlie. You had no idea this would happen and you couldn't have known—"

"Yes, I could." He cut her off and blew out a harsh breath, his expression growing even more remote. Remote and angry. "I should have known. The threats directed at the family are all being investigated, vetted, and security tightened."

"But they didn't threaten Richard." She understood guilt and pain, but she couldn't imagine what was going through his mind in this moment. "You can only work what you know."

"What I know?" He glared at her, and where once upon a time the frosty glaze burning in his eyes might have urged her to step back, she understood grief and pain. "What I know is that when you left, Richard was there. He is my best friend. If I need him, he comes. If I need his advice, he always offers it—hell, even when I don't."

As quickly as the fury bloomed, it quelled again.

"He would not have been on that road today if I hadn't needed—"

*If you hadn't needed to talk about me.* He didn't say it and he didn't have to. She would have to be blind to not notice his withdrawal or the distrust in his gaze when he looked at her. But she packed all of that away, blocking the kneejerk prick of pain stabbing her heart. She didn't deserve his trust yet, but he needed her.

"Let me ask you this—if Richard or you realized the danger, do you think he wouldn't have come?" She moistened her lips. Pushing may not be what he needed, but Charlie rarely backed down and even when she knew him in college, he was more critical of himself than anyone else.

He rubbed her hand between his palms and shook his head slowly. "No. He wouldn't take security if I threw it at him either. He likes to roam and security is extra baggage." His lips twisted into a rueful smile. "He traveled with me one summer, between his years at law school. We hadn't managed to talk much that year—and he needed a change of pace. He said he preferred law school afterwards."

The snort of laughter wasn't much, but the lost look on his face faded. "After my father passed, I had to tour all of our properties. It's far more extensive than many realize...more even than I knew. That year we went to Belgium, India, Egypt, and Australia."

"Australia?" That was a new one. What could his family have there?

"A sheep station. It's in the middle of nowhere. We flew into Sydney, then another plane to a small airport on the edge of the outback and cars to the station. We had to travel with about eight security guards, two for each vehicle, and then Richard was assigned a personal detail while he vacationed with me. You have never heard so many complaints. He kept trying to slip his guards—testing them he called it. But later—later he told me he hated feeling watched all the time, even when they were discreet. He *knew* they were there."

Gradually, he sat back, still holding her hand, and she scooted to stay with him. "I'm sure his detail didn't enjoy him trying to wander away." She didn't know Kyle very well, but she could imagine that fierce expression if she tried similar antics.

"They made a game out of it. Richard likes to play cards and so do the guards. So if he won enough hands, they didn't have to pay up if they didn't lose him."

Anna's mouth opened. "Good grief. Did they lose him?"

"Once." Charlie nodded, a quick smile passing over his lips like summer lightning slashing the sky.

She admitted to being suitably impressed. She couldn't even leave the tower without the elevator stopping at the security floor. "Were they very mad?"

"Oh, they were." Charlie reached up to rub the back of his neck. "Furious. But they paid up without complaint...and he never managed it again."

"How did he do it?"

Charlie shook his head. "He never told me. Said it was a trade secret." A small smile fastened to his mouth. "But Rick was the clever one—he used to find ways to sneak women in and out of the dorm, bring in a coffee cart or a kegger..."

"I remember." Anna smiled a little. "I believe he even snuck me in once or twice—just for your birthday."

He cut his glance up at her then and surprised pleasure rippled across his face. "I forgot about that."

"I wanted to do something special for you, but it was spring and you took three extra classes —and you were in the library nearly every night." She'd almost forgotten this until he mentioned Richard's habit. "He had me put on a pizza-de-livery uniform and I got past the RA, delivered the pizza and traded outfits with the girl in the room..."

"Girl in the room?" Charlie frowned.

"Oh yeah, Richard had his party while you were studying." She grinned. "I think her name was Melody? Melanie? Melissa? I don't know. But she was about my height and weight. We traded clothes and she took off."

"You traded clothes while Richard was in the room?" Charlie's brows drew together.

"Yes—but he stared at the wall the whole time and I was perfectly respectable un-derneath."

"In the black lace cups and thong?" He snorted.

"You liked it."

"That, I did." He let go of her hand and slid an arm around her waist and pulled her closer. She snuggled up to his shoulder and sighed.

"He can't die, Anna."

"He won't." She believed that. "He's good at sneaking in and out trouble, he'll get out of this."

They lapsed into silence, Charlie's chin resting against her hair. The clock ticked off the interminable seconds. Two hours passed before the door opened again and the doctor appeared. Anna blinked away the hazy doze and sat forward so Charlie could rise.

"Your Highness, Mr. Prentiss is being moved to recovery now. Everything went well, we did remove his spleen and we've managed to stop all the other bleeds. It will be a few hours before you can see him and we'll know more tomorrow about his prognosis, but it looks good—very good—right now."

Charlie's shoulders sagged briefly and he bowed his head. "Thank you, Doctor. We will stay here until we can see him."

The doctor looked like she wanted to say more, but she refrained and left. Anna reached up to touch his hand, but he pulled away and slid the hand into his pockets. "I need to call Barbara now. I can have Kyle take you back to the penthouse. You should get some sleep."

And just like that, the door between them closed.

~

## ARMAND

It was well past dawn before Armand made it back to the penthouse. Anna refused to leave, even when he spoke at length with Richard's sister, his attending surgeons, and security. She waited for him, staying in the secure surgical floor waiting room. He managed to coax her into going home to sleep only after she extracted a promise that he would be along directly.

He left his coat and tie in the car, but security would send both up later. He sat with Richard until the attorney's eyes opened. He wouldn't likely remember it, but Armand would. Peterson arranged for a detail to remain at the hospital. Richard's aversion to security aside—he would be in the hospital for several days if not weeks and Armand refused to leave him unguarded.

Pausing at the bar, Armand poured himself a drink and tossed it back. Exhaustion wore at him. He'd leaned hard on Anna tonight and she kept him going. He couldn't believe he forgot about his birthday—arriving to find her waiting for him in his bed—right down to the bow. He poured a second drink and carried it with him. The apartment was silent, and he stopped at her bedroom door and ran his fingers down the wood. He wanted to open it and go inside to her.

Trusting her didn't seem so distant a concept after the night—but she wasn't safe with him. Dragging his fingers away, he rubbed his face.

They needed to put more resources into tracking down Richard's attacker and eliminating this threat. If it meant declaring on Belarian television that he slept with goats, he needed that party to stop lobbying for his family's return. Opening the door to his room, he found that a lamp burned next to the bed—low and friendly. Unbuttoning his shirt with one hand and balancing his drink with the other, he paused.

Anna lay sound asleep in the middle of his bed, curled on her side. His heart squeezed. Her dark hair spread over the pillows, deep shadows of fatigue smudged under her eyes. Quiet and slow, he walked over and set his drink down on the nightstand. A note propped against the clock actually dragged a weary smile from him.

*It's not your birthday, but I'm here anyway.*

He stripped off his clothes, drained the drink and crawled in next to her. She rolled over and snuggled right into his arms. Even in sleep, she fit against him perfectly. His eyes drifted closed, he hadn't thought sleep was possible when he left the hospital. But Richard was alive and Anna was in his arms.

*It's a lot better than a birthday.*

# CHAPTER 16
## ANNA

She woke up to delicious tension coiling through her. Her body hummed with need.

His hands glided over her breasts, massaging, and his mouth followed. Every caress fluttered through her and when he sank into her, she arched up to meet him. Charlie's mouth fastened over hers and they rocked together, riding the demanding rhythm until they surged together and tumbled over the precipice.

An hour later, they sat at the breakfast table. The thoughtful staff had left them a cold buffet of bagels, muffins and Danishes. The coffee was hot and fresh. Twice she caught him staring at her with raw, naked emotion in his eyes, but the look would shutter when their gazes collided. The next three days followed the same pattern. Every night she would go to bed alone—in his bed. The repeat of their past in Norway wasn't lost on her. She might go to his bed alone, but the difference was he woke her in the night, always making love to her—a desperation and need in his touch that left her aching to fill the empty places inside him.

But as close as their nights brought them, the days pushed them apart. They shared breakfast and then he would disappear into his office, to go to the hospital, to meet with the FBI. She learned belatedly that his brothers were no longer in residence at the tower, having been whisked away to the airport sometime in the night after Richard's accident. Alyx called and left a message—she and Daniel would not be present during the opening fundraiser for the scholarship. She apologized, but her husband surprised her with a tropical second honeymoon to parts unknown.

She would be in touch. The sense of isolation grew. Anna kept her distance from her family, and Charlie cleared the decks.

The tension in the security staff heightened. She went to the hospital twice, always under heavy guard. The number of men on her detail increased the closer they came to the event night —because she was on-site meeting with event coordinators, inspecting the party setup, and a shorter trip to her house to fetch her dress, shoes and other accessories. Kyle offered to send one of his men to pick up her items, but when she pointed out they would have to go through her intimate personal belongings, he sent Kate. They were adamant that she not go, and she didn't want to argue with him.

The air was pregnant with the sense of waiting. The other shoe needed to drop. Kyle and two others followed her up the hospital hallway to

Richard's room. Two security officers stood outside the room. The LAPD maintained a uniform on scene. It turned out the police department was very fond of Richard Prentiss—she didn't realize he represented the police department in numerous lawsuits, more often than not having mediated disastrous lawsuits into public-relations wins.

Knocking once, she waited for the murmured "come in" before opening the door. Kyle glanced in first, then held the door open for her. Richard looked like hell, but four days after life-saving surgery and being tumbled around in his vehicle like a margarita shaker, he was alive.

"Good morning—or is it afternoon?" Richard gave her a polite, if vaguely warm, smile. The bruises on his face were a collection of purple and blue, fading to green and yellow at the edges. A thin row of stitches vanished into his hairline and his right wrist was in a cast. The rest of his bandages were hidden beneath the dreadfully unflattering hospital gown.

"Afternoon." Anna pulled a chair over to the side of the bed. A hint of Charlie's aftershave still lingered amid the antiseptic hospital scents. It didn't surprise her, she knew he came every single day—sometimes twice. "Actually, it's late afternoon. The party is in a few hours."

"Sorry I'm going to miss it." But the dry humor in the words amused her.

"Four times the security, press that is already camped out to catch early arrivals, and a guest list that features everything from celebrities to foreign dignitaries?" She lifted her eyebrows.

"Okay. Not that sorry." He chuckled briefly, but the laugh quickly turned to a wince and a cough. "Sorry—hurts to laugh."

"Then I'll try not to be funny." She set her purse down and clasped her hands together. She thought about this visit several times on the ride over, but she was here as much to see him and have the tangible proof that he was still with them as she was to talk to him.

"How's he doing?" Richard's gaze fixed on her steadily.

"I don't know. He's...retreating and isolating himself. I keep thinking we get a little closer and then he pushes me away again." Moistening her lips, Anna shook her head. It was so much more than that. At night, in his bed, he held her, made love to her, let her be there for him and it was perfect. But during the day, he may as well have been a million miles away. He'd erected a wall between them—a wall with no gates, no windows, no place to pass through—and she didn't know how to bring it down.

If she could.

"It's been a hard week for him." Richard leaned his head back against the pillows, his eyes drifting half-closed. She thought he drifted into sleep, but then he spoke. "Ask, Anna."

"Am I that transparent?" Guilt nibbled at her, the attorney needed to recover.

"No, but caring about him isn't always easy."

His eyes opened. "So ask. I can't promise I'll answer."

"He's pushing me away—but I don't think he wants me to go. I told him I loved him and it was perfect and magical and then cold and distant. He's giving me a million reasons to leave."

"And you are looking for one to stay?" He sighed at her slow nod. "I can't answer that for you—or for him. One of the reasons our friendship works is he trusts me to keep his confidences."

"Do I have a reason to hope? That I haven't inescapably screwed this up for us? I—I had this feeling in his office that day that he wanted something from me. And then again later... There are moments when he's Charlie and others where he's not." Anna rubbed a hand over her mouth and shook her head. "I feel like I know him so very well and at other times...he's a complete stranger."

"He's a man, Anna. He's the same man he's always been." Richard shifted in the bed, reaching for the remote, and she leaned forward to nudge it closer. He gave her a small smile of gratitude and then hit the button to sit the headrest up. His face went pale with the struggle, but he looked at her steadily. "But that's not really what you want to know."

*Does he love me?* If he did—if he loved her—that was reason enough to stay, to do everything she could to make the past up to him. To prove to him every day that she wouldn't leave this time.

*And if he doesn't...*

Then maybe they could bury all this pain between them and really get on with their lives. That thought made her ill. She'd convinced herself for years that she was better off without him.

She didn't think she could do it twice.

"I should let you rest."

"You should talk to him."

"I've tried," she snapped, then bit her lip with a grimace. "I'm sorry, it's not your fault. I have tried to talk to him. I told him I love him and every time I do he shuts down. It's like he's trying to box me up and close the walls in and keep me from getting too close. I hurt him, Rick. I know I did. I can't take back what I did—I can't give him back those ten years after I walked away. I don't even know where to start. But I love him. I want to be there for him and he won't let me."

"Don't give him the choice." Richard fell silent, a struggle playing out over his features. For all that he was a brilliant poker player, the urge to say something etched into his face. But the firm line of his mouth compressing told her he wouldn't. "I can't tell you what you want to know. Being a prince isn't easy—not for any of the brothers. You're basing a lot of what you know about the last few years on what the news reports, aren't you?"

He turned the question back on her and Anna nodded slowly. "I watched every special, reviewed the Google alerts when his name was mentioned—" Embarrassment heated her face. "I just wanted to know he was okay."

"Nothing wrong with that—but ask yourself

this. Have you watched the news reports over the last couple of weeks since the two of you saw each other again?"

The ridiculous speculation, the aborted wedding announcement from Nikole and the interviews with classmates she didn't even recall—the kernels of the truth were in the story, but they made up such a small part of it. The news stories she followed rarely reflected the information she read in the foundation guidebook or even bore a passing resemblance to the man she knew in college—the man she knew now.

"There you go." Richard closed his eyes. "Now you're thinking."

"You're a good friend, Rick."

"I'm the best." His lips curved into a fleeting half smile before his expression sobered. "Don't hurt him again, Anna. I like you—but I don't think I can forgive you twice."

Rising, she leaned forward and pressed a kiss to his cheek. "Feel better."

He patted her hand, and though she appreciated the gesture it remained an awkward moment. Richard was Charlie's guy—his best friend, his confidant, the man he trusted. They shared history, good times and bad. He'd been there when Anna hadn't.

"Have fun at the party." He gave her a small smile of encouragement.

"Oh, I'm sure it will be a blast." She left him to sleep and walked out to find Kyle and the others waiting for her. Still chewing over what she knew and what she didn't, who he was and whom the world saw.

She waited until they were in the car and leaned forward. "Kyle?"

"Yes, ma'am?"

"How long have you worked for Ch—the prince?"

"About five years, ma'am. Usually his American stops, but occasionally in Europe."

"Can I ask you a question?" She nibbled the inside of her lip.

"Of course. I can't promise to answer it, though. Discretion is inherent to our position." He gave her an easy smile, but she understood. They'd explained this to her from the beginning —they would never discuss what she did or said in their presence, she had to trust them implicitly for the security team to be able to protect her.

She thought about the question long and hard. "Has the prince ever provided a private security detail for the women he's dated?"

They were passing through downtown on the way back to the tower before Kyle answered. "When they travel with him, they are usually under his security detail. But a private detail for them directly? No, ma'am. Not that I'm aware of."

Anna leaned back. Charlie was Prince Armand. Prince Armand was Charlie. He didn't share that part of himself with the rest of the world—he'd reserved Charlie for her. He'd assigned a protection detail to her.

He was offering her a million reasons to leave. *Is he afraid of me—or for me?*

But she only needed one reason—him—to stay.

"Are you still planning to arrive at the event center at five p.m., Miss Novak?"

"Yes, I am. As long as security is comfortable with that." She needed a perfect time to prove to him that she loved him—all of him. Charlie and Armand both. She wanted this relationship, she loved him, she craved him and she needed to show him. Tonight was the first step, with all the pressure and hell he was under, she wouldn't repeat the mistakes of their past.

She caught sight of the tower in the distance and for the first time, she didn't see a glass prison or lofty palace in the sky. She saw home. Excitement and anticipation fluttered in her belly. It wouldn't be easy—her prince was a stubborn, stubborn man.

*But I'm no pushover... He can try to shut me out, but time crumbles all walls...*

~

## ARMAND

The FBI arrived at the tower on Armand's way out. Security called down to the car and they drove back to the elevator to meet the pair of agents. Thomason, the senior agent Armand spoke to the day of Richard's accident, and his partner, Fitch, looked pleased—well, as pleased as two federal agents might.

"Your Highness, thank you for meeting us,

we'll try not to keep you." Thomason led the discussion and held out his phone with a photograph on it. The man resembled Yuri Markov, save for the conspicuous lack of tattoos.

"This is Dmitri Markov, Yuri's younger brother. Not sure how he slipped our net, but we picked him up at LAX yesterday afternoon on an outbound flight for Belaria. His rental car was in long-term parking and contained long-range photographic equipment."

Armand studied the man's expression. There was a vacant emptiness in Markov's eyes. He rarely saw up close those who would hurt him and his family. Violence surged through him. "Has he confessed?"

"No. But he was here on a forged passport, the name didn't match his and we have enough to hold him. Fortunately, he didn't think to clean out his car—the man was a slob—and we found receipts to three different motels. His brother Yuri was staying at one until two days ago. Now he's in the wind, but we know where he was and we're putting together a profile on where he's been so we can anticipate where he might be next."

Returning Agent Thomason's phone, Armand frowned. "So we have one in custody, and one still at large."

"As far as we can tell. We'd like to ask you to not attend your event tonight. Keep a low profile for a few days and let us track this guy down."

"Absolutely not." He had no intentions of keeping a low profile. If Yuri Markov wanted to kill an Andraste, he would have one single target to focus on: Armand. His security was ready—even if they didn't approve.

"Your Highness..." Fitch interjected. "We can't guarantee your safety. While there have been no new threats issued, the presence of yourself and Miss Novak at the same event—whatever is setting these guys off, if they want to make a statement, this is where they will do it."

His gut clenched. Anna had left an hour earlier. Peterson assured him they'd doubled her detail for the night and Kyle Johnson would be at her side at all times along with two female bodyguards. They would keep her safe and after tonight... After tonight the bull's-eye he'd painted on her back would be gone.

"Thank you for your concern, gentlemen. But we postponed this event once, we will be proceeding as planned. We've taken security into account. Please let me know what happens with Markov." At least they got the bastard who hurt Richard. It was a small recompense for his friend's injuries, but better than leaving the man at large.

In the car again, Armand motioned for the driver to get them under way. He still had three stops to make before the event center. He glanced at his watch. They would arrive after the official beginning, but he planned the timing for maximum attention.

～

## ANNA

*"We are coming to you live from the Cross Concert Hall and Event Center here in Los Angeles where the Andraste Grand Duke, Prince Armand, is hosting a gala to launch the Princess Alyxandretta Dagmar Scholarship. This is a fund dedicated to foster children who might not otherwise be able to afford college. Hosting this event alongside the prince is Miss Anna Novak, the administrative director for the fund and, according to many reports, the prince's first love. The two reunited recently after a near ten-year separation. All royal watchers will be on this couple tonight—could another royal wedding be in the offing?"*

ANNA SMOOTHED a hand down the velvet-and-silk royal-blue dress. It cost her over five hundred dollars and was worth every penny. The snug bodice emphasized her curves, while the flaring skirt gave it an air of whimsy. She wore very simple jewelry and sedate cosmetics. This event was about the scholarship, not her. Her hair gathered back from her face and spilled down from a simple knot in the back. She'd let the curls do their thing and practiced her smile in the mirror while she got ready.

She'd hoped to see Charlie before she left, but he'd been on a call in his office and left word to not be disturbed. But she suspected Charlie knew the color of her dress, because a black velvet box waited for her on her bed. She glanced down at her wrist and smiled at the sapphire and diamond bracelet. It was simple, elegant—and utterly unexpected. More so was the note with it. *You will be magnificent tonight, never forget you are a treasure.*

He confused the hell out of her.

She arrived early enough to walk the ballroom. Kyle and his men wore tuxedos, blending in with the crowd—not that their six-foot-plus statures, square jaws and broad shoulders weren't noticeable, but she understood. They each wore flesh-colored earbuds, and if she hadn't known what to look for, she might have overlooked it.

*Better to let them do their jobs while I do mine.* The guests began trickling in at five after seven. Required to pass through two checkpoints, they were greeted by waitstaff offering champagne flutes. Anna agreed to mingle on one side of the room only, away from the main entrance, and it didn't take her long to be drawn into conversations with a dozen different guests. She shook hands, talked about the scholarship and received numerous pledges.

Kate attended alongside her, thankfully. She carried a digital tablet, took personal information, noting the donation numbers and more. Anna's head whirled as they moved through the crowd. The turnout was enormous. Of the twelve hundred guests invited, Kate told her over seven hundred were in attendance. Since they were charging a thousand dollars a plate, they had already earned a huge amount for the fund.

At exactly a quarter to eight, a stir rolled through the crowd and Anna turned from greeting the head of a movie studio to see Charlie arriving. The nervous flutters in her stomach doubled, then plummeted.

He wasn't alone.

The Grand Duke Armand made a hell of a noise when he entered the crowded ballroom with not one, but three women—including his former paramour Nikole holding on to his right arm. He looked devastating in his black tuxedo, his charming smile lighting up his dark looks. His hair feathered rakishly across his forehead. Instantly captivated, the crowd surged toward him.

Men shook his hand. Women curtsied. Photographers snapped his picture. The buxom blonde model on his arm looked across the room, her gaze cutting into Anna's with a look of such utter triumph in her brittle smile.

Stomach aching, Anna forced her own smile to stay in place. When Armand seemingly glanced across the room at her, he spared her the briefest of nods. She returned it, trying to ignore the sucker-punched feeling in her abdomen and the cascade of hot, then cold, racing over her skin.

The executive seemed to sense her distraction and excused himself. Anna glanced at Kyle. "I need a moment," she murmured.

He nodded and with one gesture, her security fell in around her and they began to weave their way through the crowd toward the side of the room. Kate, swept up by the security force, stayed with her. "Are you all right, Anna?"

"I'm fine." Anna lied through her teeth. "I just need to catch my breath and maybe splash some water on my face."

At the restroom, Kyle opened the door and Kate slipped in to check for him. "It's empty."

Anna followed her inside, grateful for the sudden silence away from the murmuring crowd. She planted her hands against the cool marble and closed her eyes. Breathing through her nose and out her mouth, she tried to calm the wild stampede in her chest. He brought Nikole. It didn't matter that those other women were with him with their poured-on dresses and glittering jewels and overwhelmingly gorgeous bodies—he'd brought Nikole.

The woman who name-dropped him as her fiancé. The woman with whom he'd shared an on-again, off-again affair.

Was it suddenly on-again?

Nausea surged up and she pressed her lips together. She would not get sick. She would not do this.

A cool washcloth draped against the back of her neck and she jerked, glancing up to find Kate looking at her in the mirror. "You're not okay."

"I am fine. But thank you. I just—"

"Need a moment, you said." Quiet empathy echoed in the woman's voice. "What can I do?"

Anna looked at herself in the mirror and saw a pair of hollow eyes gazing back at her. She took another lungful of air and exhaled. "How are we doing with donations?" Focus on the job. *We're here to raise money, a lot of those people came to gape and point at the royal sideshow...but they're paying for the privilege. Hold on to that.*

"Well, in addition to the per-plate fee, of which we take half directly for the scholarship and the checks and pledges we've taken so far..." Kate glanced down at her digital tablet. "About four million, five hundred thousand. And we've only spoken to about a fourth of the people in attendance. I'm sure there will be more after your speech..."

*Oh God.* Nausea burned up again and she barely made it into the toilet in time to throw up. Kate was there again, holding her dress and hair out of the way. She didn't hesitate, disappearing to the sink and returning with another cold washcloth.

"I'll get you some water." She walked over to the door and had some quiet words with Kyle. By the time she returned, Anna was back at the sink and rinsing out her mouth. Thankfully, she didn't soil her dress. Kate passed her a cold glass with ice and water in it. She also held two tablets in her hand.

"They're for motion sickness. It's not quite anxiety, but they should help. Just don't drink any more wine or champagne."

The thought of alcohol revolted Anna. She took the pills and washed them down with the water.

Kate leaned against the counter. "Can I give you some advice?"

"You just watched me throw up and freak out." Anna blotted the damp washcloth against her mouth and pulled open her clutch to find something to repair her makeup with. "I think you've earned the right to give me some advice."

"His Highness is a prince, a grand duke, CEO of a large international corporation and sits on numerous boards and advisory councils in the European Union. He's wealthy, famous, a celebrity of sorts, and really not hard on the eyes." Kate ticked off the qualities with her rounded, red nails.

"I'm pretty much aware of that." Being reminded only made her unease sink its claws deeper into her belly.

"Of course you are." Kate smiled. "But you've forgotten the most important part."

"That is?" Irritation crept into her voice. The woman had become something of a friend over the last couple of weeks, but she didn't know Charlie—not the way Anna did.

"He's a man, sweetie. And all men are stupid." Kate's quick grin was equal parts amused and sympathetic. "I don't know why he brought the freak shows with him, but he isn't paying any attention to them. He watched you when he came in that room. He knew exactly where you were and when you left, his gaze followed you all the way out. So you go out there, you put on your game face and you show him exactly why he can't take his eyes off you."

Anna gaped. "He's your boss."

"That doesn't make him any less male or any

less prone to their fits of stupidity." Kate turned to the mirror and leaned forward to check her teeth. "Besides...you look amazing, you do amazing work and you've been busting your ass to get this event off the ground. It's your night—take it. Now, fix your lipstick, dab some perfume on and let's go knock them all dead."

"You're right," Anna said after a long silence.

"Of course I am." Kate winked and gave her arm a friendly pat. "You ready for it?"

*Not even a little. I'd rather go have my teeth extracted than walk back out there.*

"No, but let's do it anyway." Anna fixed her smile, burying the hurt beneath a veneer of professionalism. She would do it. She would give the crowd a show—maybe not the romantic love story they came seeking, but she would make the most of the opportunity to fill the scholarship fund's coffers and raise enough money to send a thousand kids to the colleges of their choice.

She could get through the next few hours.

*Right?*

# CHAPTER 17
# ARMAND

"*In what may be the most shocking turn of events this evening, the Andraste Grand Duke, Armand, arrived at the Event Center almost forty-five minutes late for the gala he is hosting with not only another woman on his arm, but three women, including internationally renowned Nikole. As you may recall, just a week ago, Nikole 'announced' that she and the prince were engaged. She later retracted that statement, but with her unexpected appearance at her side tonight, could the reunited love affair with Anna Novak be over already? They don't call him the playboy prince for nothing. Back to you, Kym.*"

ANNA DISAPPEARED LONG ENOUGH that Armand began to worry. Glad-handing his way through the crowd, he headed in the direction she disappeared. Pulling free of Nikole, he sent her off to mingle and find a drink. He was halfway across the ballroom when Anna reentered. Her chin up, she didn't look in his direction at all. Her dazzling smile focused on the British ambassador and his wife. She shook hands, gestured to some of the prints hanging around the room that detailed the scholarship and moved on.

Relieved that she was okay, he turned his attention to the New York bankers seeking a deal with Dagmar International. It never failed to surprise him how many corporate heads would attend a charity event as a negotiating tactic. The next thirty minutes passed in tedium. Per his instructions, his personal security maintained a discreet distance, allowing him to flow through the crowd.

Two representatives from Belaria actually put in an appearance, the middle Kachusov son and his attaché. "Your Highness, it is good to see you looking so well." His tone disagreed with the words.

"Colonel—isn't it?" Armand enjoyed the look of surprise rippling across Kachusov's face. He didn't wear a uniform, but the prince made it a point to know his enemies.

"Yes, Your Highness. Although I am retired presently."

"Ah, but the life of a military man is never complete unless his country has need of him again." They shook hands briefly. "Thank you for contributing to the cause. My cousin will be thrilled by the outpouring of international support for something so close to her heart." Years of practice kept his smile firm and his tone even. He stared into the eyes of a man who may have sent death threats to his family—or at least instigated them.

"It is a sad event to know that even princesses can grow up in abject poverty. My family wept for yours when you were at long last reunited." The colonel touched a hand to his chest over his heart. "Though we were surprised that you allowed her to marry a commoner such as Daniel Voldakov."

"Love knows no caste system and nor should it. Will you be writing a check to the fund tonight? I would be happy to take your donation." He accepted a glass of champagne from the bodyguard working in the waitstaff.

"Forgive me, sir, but one wouldn't expect you to... What is the American colloquialism? Panhandle for funds?" Kachusov's aide's thinly veiled contempt certainly needed some work.

"I do not think any job is too menial when the cause is precious. And I have nothing to prove—" he fixed his gaze on Kachusov, "—to anyone in *any* country about my intentions or otherwise. I am a content man when I can serve the needs of others—sending foster children to university is a worthy cause. As are all causes that the Dagmar Foundation champions."

"I see. So you enjoy the simple pleasures and aren't looking to create new ones?" The man studied him, doubt clear in his expression.

"None."

Nikole chose that moment to breeze up to him and wrap an arm around him. He settled a hand on her hip and smiled at Kachusov. "And what more pleasures could I need than these?" He switched to Russian, because he had no interest in encouraging Nikole's behavior further than what suited the situation.

"Excuse me." The silky thread of Anna's voice cascaded through the room's sound system. Conversations halted and eyes turned toward the stage. Anna stood there, smiling and graceful. "I wanted to take a moment to thank each and every one of you for joining us this evening and to our host, the Andraste Grand Duke for his generosity reflected in this event. In a few moments, we will invite you into the next room for dinner and a small presentation about the scholarship fund. For those of you that have already opened your hearts and your wallets to support the Princess Alyxandretta Dagmar Scholarship, I cannot thank you enough, but by your very presence here tonight you are sending a clear message that everyone deserves the opportunity to fly."

Her gaze landed on him, like a butterfly, gentle and seemingly serene, before moving on. Even the quietest of whispers faded as they listened.

"My parents had six children—all of us big dreamers with huge plans because they encouraged us to seize every opportunity, to fight for what we believed was right and to take risks. With risk comes great reward and sometimes great disappointment. But whether you have a lot of money or none, what truly makes a difference is having the support of people who believe in you."

She licked her lips, the gesture so open and vulnerable could captivate even the hardest of hearts. "I learned the hard way that support comes in all shapes and sizes. It comes from telling the truth...and sometimes from lying. It comes from meaning well and wanting the best... To doing what is right and what is just. It comes from walking away when nothing else can be done and staying to fight even when all hope is lost. I learned that education is more than facts and figures, history, and dates. It's discovering who you are—because that is the person you will always be—even when the world batters you, challenges you, tries to tear you down and build you up—" She swallowed hard.

Nikole leaned over to murmur in his ear and he silenced her with a look. She withdrew her arm and backed away a step. On the stage Anna collected herself. "This scholarship says that hope is never lost and even if you don't know who you are yet, I—" she stretched her hand to the crowd, "—*we* believe in you. We know you can be the person you were meant to be, the person you can be, and we will support you in your choices and your decisions."

He didn't imagine it. She looked right at him.

"Trust is a leap of faith. Tonight, we are trusting these students to take these advantages and leap with them as they become who they were meant to be. Thank you very much."

Applause rose to deafening levels and Anna

swiped at her cheek and smiled as she turned to shake hands with a dozen well-wishers. They closed in on the stage, but her security was there and they kept them from getting too close in larger than groups of one or two.

"Many men would follow a woman like that," Kachusov said in Russian, resuming their conversation as if it hadn't been interrupted.

"Perhaps, but she has no desire to lead—only help those less fortunate." He dragged his gaze away and fought to keep a bored look on his face. "Which is not as much fun as she makes it sound. If you gentlemen will excuse me..." He strolled away, his skin crawling with a thousand ants nibbling at him. He wanted to go over and sweep Anna up in his arms, congratulate her on the brilliant speech. But dismissing her publicly—it would protect her.

And he wanted her alive more.

~

## ANNA

"Are you ready to go in?" Kyle slipped up to stand right at her elbow. The doors on the other end of the grand ballroom opened and guests began to filter in to their tables.

"In a minute." She'd managed to keep from searching the room for the last hour, but when she'd looked at Charlie during the speech, a pulse went through her. For those few seconds, they connected—really connected. Gaze skimming the crowd, she searched for him now. When she located him, he stood near the entrance—alone.

As in *without his security* alone.

*What is he doing? Where are they?*

Frowning, she picked up her skirt and started forward. A series of popping noises bounced beneath the noise of the crowd. Anna didn't make it another step. Kyle's hand locked on her arm and suddenly she was up off the ground and going backward. Armand disappeared out the door and three security suits surged forward.

"Wait." She fought Kyle's arm, but he didn't slow. Kate was right in front of her—and Anna barely had time to process the fact that her "assistant" had a gun. Three additional guards closed around them. They didn't slow until they were out a side door and she was tucked into a car. Kyle slipped into the front seat.

"What's going on?" She couldn't swallow the sour taste of fear in her throat or banish the quaver from her voice.

Kate stared at her for a half second. "Novak secure." She closed the door and banged the roof. They were leaving their own party.

"Kyle." She reached forward to touch the seat. "What happened?"

"Shots fired. Hang on..." He clearly listened to whatever chatter happened on his earbud. The SUV swung around a hard corner and she held on to the seat to stay upright.

Charlie was by himself.

He'd arrived with a gaggle of old girlfriends.

He'd ignored her.

But that moment...that moment during her speech when she'd looked at him—she didn't imagine that.

*He made himself the target...*

She closed her eyes as they swung around another corner. He was so upset about Richard. He sent his brothers away. He must have arranged to sweep Alyx out of the country. He buried her in guards—her "loaned" assistant apparently had been one too.

And he walked through that crowd alone, unguarded and highly visible.

*Please let him be okay.*

"Roger that, we're taking Miss Novak back to the tower right now." Kyle gave her a small smile. "They have the shooter in custody."

Heart squeezing in her chest, she nodded. "Charlie?"

"His Highness will be fine. They are securing the location, Kate will continue to take donations, but for now we need to get you back to the tower." The guard turned around in the seat and faced forward. Anna exhaled a low breath. Charlie did it all to lure out the person or persons issuing the threats.

He put himself in danger to protect his family.

Rubbing a hand against her face, she stared out at the passing night. She didn't think her heart would slow until she had her arms around him—hell, she didn't even know if she would kiss him or throttle him for being so careless with his own life.

*Please don't be hurt...*

~

# ARMAND

"It's him, Your Highness." The FBI's arrival on-site so close on the heels of Markov's attempt couldn't be coincidence. They didn't care for Armand's choice to play bait, but they'd definitely taken advantage of it.

Armand nodded slowly. "Peterson said no one was hurt, can you confirm that?"

Thomason nodded. "Your man is correct. Markov waited until Miss Novak was on stage and the attention focused on her. He's apparently been here most of the evening just waiting for you." The agent gestured to the area cordoned off by crime-scene tape. "He stationed himself behind those planters, dressed like one of the staff."

"How did he get a gun past our security scanners?" Peterson and a circle of seven of his private security arrayed around Armand—with Anna off-site, they'd closed ranks on the prince.

"Plastic—high-tensile and quality plastic. It wasn't good for more than three shots. But he walked right through the metal detector with it." Thomason shook his head. "We have more than enough to hold him, but hopefully—hopefully that resolves all of this."

Armand doubted it. It ended the Markov threat, but not the family behind it. No, the family behind that threat stood inside. He hadn't missed the colonel staring at him during the speech or his lingering after the shots were fired. Only a few guests heard the pops, but security took the shooter down as soon as he lifted the gun.

The agent excused himself and Armand watched the cleanup. The grand ballroom doors were closed now, and if they managed to sweep this up swiftly, it would be a great mystery for the press to titillate the masses.

"Shall we get you back to the tower, Your Highness?" Peterson motioned toward the side exit, but Armand shook his head.

"No. We still have a purpose here." The Kachusov colonel still attended. If he disappeared on the heels of Anna, it gave her more import to them. Besides, what man in his right mind lingered at an event where someone tried to kill him?

"Sir, if you don't mind some candor?" Peterson waited.

"I never mind candor from you."

"Good. Please end this foolish gesture and go back to the tower with Miss Novak. She's probably scared and worried about you. Staying here doesn't send her a message you would want her to receive."

No. It sent exactly the right message. It encouraged her to go, far away from him where she could be safe. "Let me know when she arrives at the tower."

"And if she asks about you?"

He died a little inside. "Tell her I am dancing."

Peterson shook his head, but Armand returned to the dining room as the video presentation about the scholarship ended. The applause was rich and enthusiastic. A live band set up and soon the wine flowed and the music played. He lost count of the number of women he danced with, paying each one courteous attention. He stayed for the entire event, leaving only when the caterers shooed the stragglers out the door so they could clean up.

Exhaustion wore on him on the ride back to the tower. He checked in with the hospital. Richard continued to improve. Peterson informed him that no new threats came in and the chatter with regard to Anna seemed to have muted.

He closed his eyes and leaned his head back against the seat.

～

*"You know, Amy, tonight has been one filled with surprises. Sources inside the royal circle are now suggesting that the relationship between Anna Novak and Prince Armand was entirely fabricated. The couple did not spend any time together tonight, and aside from thanking him in her speech, they didn't discuss each other. Miss Novak left the event early due to a mild illness. A source on her staff mentioned she was extremely anxious about speaking in front of such a large crowd and may have been overwhelmed. Hardly princess material when you think about it. Fortunately for the ladies, the playboy prince continued in fine form long into the night after Novak*

*left the gala, dancing with every eligible lady in the house. Poor Nikole, though, a tantrum earned her an early exit from the event—I would hazard a guess that the prince didn't make any lady happy tonight. This is Jill Roberts, Celebrity News."*

# CHAPTER 18
# ARMAND

H e spent an hour going over the security's performance during the gala and offering his congratulations—and thanks—for their swift, decisive actions. They hadn't wanted Armand to play the target or to bait out the assassin, but he'd insisted. Of all the choices he'd made since inheriting his father's title, this one brought him the least joy for the greatest sacrifice. He wanted his family safe.

*All of them.*

Time would tell if the Kachusov representative took the hints and their failure and let go of the vendetta. He would also have to deal with George and keep him too busy to fund any more political nonsense and in six months or a year it would all quiet down. Maybe—just maybe—he could crawl back to Anna at that point. Loosening his tie, he walked out of the elevator and down the hall to the penthouse.

The main rooms were dark, illuminated only by the moon outside the lights of the city beyond.

Two steps into the room, a hiss of air was his only warning before something struck him in the forehead. Wincing, he peered into the darkness. The hiss of air repeated in rapid succession and three more solid thunks hit him in the chest.

"What the hell?"

Falling back to the front door, he hit the wall switch and brought up the lights.

Anna stood on the sofa, a Nerf gun in her hand, and she fired it again. The rapid-fire autoloader was straight out of his own collection, used for playing with children. She pelted him with darts.

"Anna!" They didn't actually hurt, startling him more than anything. He strode across the room before she could reload it and pulled it out of her hands. "What are you doing?"

She growled—actually growled—and grabbed a pillow from the sofa and struck him. It bounced off his shoulder and fluffed his hair. But the second swipe caught his cheek and he actually fell back a step.

"Are. You. Out. Of. Your. Mind?" She punctuated every word with a blow of the pillow. He grabbed for it and wrestled it out of her hands, but she raced away to grab another one and threw it at him.

He ducked and chased after her, surprised as hell that after the night he'd had, he could smile. "Anna—stop."

She picked up a lamp and hurled it. It went wide and smashed against the wall and took his smile with it. He barely managed to dodge the next set of missiles. A picture frame followed, then a vase. When she grabbed a marble egg he held up both hands. "Anna, darling—" Good God, she was fierce and beautiful.

The front door opened and Armand caught sight of Kyle filling the entryway. Anna looked at him. "Out. We are having a private discussion. I promise I'm not going to kill him."

Kyle flicked a look from Armand to Anna and back again. "I'll be outside."

And he closed the door.

"You're upset," Armand began in a placating tone, he needed to calm her down.

"Am I really? Why would that be?" She passed the marble egg back and forth between her right and left hands. "Could it be the women you decided to parade at the party? Or maybe it was the shedding of your security so you could be a target? Or better yet, it was the not calling me yourself to tell me you were okay and spending the rest of your evening dancing like some gigolo?" Her voice cracked at the end and she slammed the egg down on the table.

The plan had been to push her away, but he couldn't handle her hurt or her loss. He blew out a breath. Time. If he bought them some time, they could make it work. "Sweetheart."

"Oh no, you can go back to Miss Novak right now. I'm pretty pissed at you." She folded her arms. "Your Hind Ass."

He blinked slowly. "What did you just say?"

"You heard me, it's slightly more polite than jackass, but since we were all playing parts tonight, I'll give you—" she made a show of looking at her wrist, a wrist that still bore the sapphire and diamond bracelet he'd left her, "—five minutes to try and spin this your way."

Gaping at her, he tried to pull together the train of thought he rode into this mess on. Her eyes sparkled, her cheeks flushed and her hair in wild disarray—as though she'd run her fingers through it a hundred times. "You're beautiful."

"Oh no, you do not get off that easily. Compliments will get you nowhere." He started forward and she backed away, circling the sofa to elude him. "You owe me an explanation, mister."

She was amazing, like the furies of old come to avenge her own honor, she railed at him. "You really are very beautiful, I'm only sorry I didn't get to tell you sooner."

"Charlie, focus on the problem at hand. We're not talking fashion," she snapped, that volatile little growl in her voice, and he couldn't help but grin.

"I don't recall you having this much of a temper before." This dark, passionate side fascinated him.

"I don't recall you ever giving me this much grief before either. What were you thinking? Risking yourself like that? Why?"

"Sweetheart, it was safe. My men knew exactly what I was doing." He continued around the sofa. "I told them about it—we needed the focus on me and the only way to do that was to take the focus off you." He caught her arms and pulled her close. "I'm sorry it scared you."

She was stiff in his arms. "You were stupid and foolish and—"

He kissed her, hard and slow. She fisted her hands against his shirt, then her mouth softened and opened to him. He was a drowning man gasping for air. How the hell was he ever going to let her go?

Breaking the kiss, he rested his forehead against hers. "I am a jackass, but I'm a jackass who loves you. The next few months—they're going to be hard, but if everything calms down then we can—" even the idea of leaving her for so short a time sank the knife in a little deeper, "—we can start to see each other again."

Drawing back, she stared up at him. "I'm sorry, what?"

"Did you mean what you said earlier? About trust...being a leap of faith?"

"Yes and don't change the subject. What do you mean in a few months we can start seeing each other again?" Her eyes narrowed and her fingers dug into his shirt.

"It's—it's not safe right now. For you. It may never be safe. It's a lot of politics and misdirection, but they are targeting you because of me. If you go back to your life and I to mine, we can give it all time to quiet down. And then—"

"Oh. Hell. No." She slapped his chest and he grimaced at the sting. "You are not making choices for me. Not anymore. You took away my choice when you didn't tell me the truth and I took away yours when I walked out all those years ago. But I'm not leaving—throw me out if you want to—but I am not going. Not this time."

A laugh worked its way up and he shook his head. "This is ridiculous."

"I'm glad we agree." Sharpness punctuated her tone.

"You didn't want this life—"

"No, I didn't know what I wanted except for one thing and that's actually never changed." She lifted her hands to his face, gentle as a feather, and stood up on her tiptoes. "You. I loved you then and I love you now. I wanted *you*—I wanted Charlie. But what I didn't realize is that I wanted Armand too. I want all of you—not just the pieces. I want to be there when you have to stand up to bullies and I want to be there when you play a video game. I gave up ten years with you because I was stupid, I will not give up ten minutes more because someone else is stupid. I know you don't trust me or think you can and..."

Tilting his head he watched her fight to find the words and touched his own fingers to her lips. "I know you don't want to change the subject, but I need the answer to this. Did you mean what you said on that stage? About trust?"

"Yes. It's a leap of faith—it's why it's so hard to get back when you've lost it. I thought I lost it when I thought I didn't know you. I didn't trust —I didn't trust that maybe you showed me who you really were all those years and that a title isn't anything more than a nuisance. I don't know if I can ever—"

"Shh." He dragged her closer and wrapped his

arms around her. He didn't know if he could make that leap—just that he wanted to. "You don't have to prove anything. Anna, this is a mess and I want you safe. I want you safe more than I want my own life."

"I don't want to be safe if it means not being with you—that's not safe, Armand. That's lonely." She said "Armand" the same way she said "Charlie," ripe with lush affection and equal parts exasperation.

"A few months, we just need a few months." He rubbed her back. "A few months to fix this."

"No."

"You're not going to change that answer, are you?" Wry, he let her go long enough to sweep her up into his arms.

"Nope. You're stuck with me."

He carried her back to the bedroom and dropped with her onto the bed. He kissed her nose. "You make me crazy."

"Well, right back at you." She ran her fingers through his hair and he dipped his head down to kiss her throat. His lips barely brushed her skin when she gave his head a tug and he winced.

"Oh no." She smiled. "You see—you came to the party with three other women." She gave him a little shove. He rolled to the side and she slid off the bed, smoothing her dress, demure as a queen. "Then you stayed to dance with a whole lot more and you still haven't agreed to not separating. So this—" she gestured to herself, "—is off-limits. I'll see you in the morning. I love you."

With that she swept out of the room. He

stared after her and didn't know whether to laugh or throw something.

What was he going to do with her?

~

## ANNA

Anna barely slept. She'd readied herself for bed, half expecting him to burst in the door at any moment. But he didn't. Rising before the alarm went off, she showered and dressed. He would try to tell her they needed to separate for a while, she would say no. He might even order her to leave—but she'd heard his declaration the night before. Yes, he was a royal jackass. But he was *her* royal ass.

*He loves me. I'm not going anywhere.*

The staff came through sometime during the night or maybe in the early hours of the morning. All the debris of her ambush had been cleaned up and breakfast set out, including scrambled eggs, toast, bacon, sausage and fried potatoes. The warmers kept the food hot and she took time to make a plate, and pour a cup of coffee before settling down with her digital tablet.

Setting the scene was important. She opened her email to see a report from Kate waiting for her on the final tally from the gala. The helpful assistant who just happened to also be a bodyguard—weren't Armand and his men clever?

*Armand.* She rolled the name around her mental palate. It wasn't as hard to think of him that way. He was still Charlie beneath. But he was also the prince. The grand duke. The head of his family. She had hours the night before to work into a good steaming mad and time to think. Once she'd got past the jealousy it wasn't hard to put two and two together. Rick knew his best friend and he'd told her to look past the news, what they reported—well, hinted that she should—and he was right.

The prince put on a grand show and she very nearly let him suck her into that vortex.

The door opened down the hall and she sat forward, picking up a piece of bacon and nibbling it as she "perused" the email report. But the first thing she saw were the zeroes and her jaw dropped.

"Good morning— What's wrong?" Armand's voice tinged heavy with concern. He walked over to the table and dropped down to crouch next to her.

"Kate sent me a report of last night's final figures..." She turned the tablet to him. "We raised fifty million dollars." The figure wasn't exact, and Kate emphasized that the accountants would give her a true and accurate statement, but fifty million dollars would send a lot of kids to school.

A hell of a lot.

"Congratulations." Armand kissed her forehead and rose. He walked over to pour himself a cup of coffee. "You were amazing last night, if I forgot to tell you."

"You did, but with all that cleavage hanging

off of you, I'm not surprised you'd forget about me."

"Anna, it was a diversion." He sighed. "I did it on purpose."

"Oh, I know." She smiled at him and took a bite out of her bacon. "I just haven't forgotten how comfortable you looked."

He carried his coffee over and hooked out the chair next to hers. Sitting down, he gave her a kind, almost soft look. She waited.

"Two months—"

"Nope." She went back to her food and flipped the email to the next note.

He drummed his fingers against the table. "You're not listening to me."

"Oh, I listened to you just fine. You're terribly worried for my safety because of a threat and you want us to take a break for a few months so the press will blow over and then *perhaps* we *might* be able to see each other..." She glanced at him.

"Exactly. It's not an ideal situation, but you would be safer."

"And in this grand plan after we take our break, do we get to see each other every other weekend? Or perhaps one weekend a month? Oh, I know, we schedule alternating holidays where we happen to encounter each other..." She paused at his consternated frown. "Seriously, that was your plan?"

"For a short while, yes." He didn't sound ter- rifically happy about her reaction to it.

She decided against throwing her coffee in his face. She rather loved his face. But the eggs would do a lot to spoil his royal dignity. "No." Flipping to the next email, she picked up her toast and took a bite.

A long huffing sigh. "You're being impossible."

"No, I'm being Anna. You're Armand. I'm Anna. We're a couple. That means we're together —not living in distant cities acting like strangers, not meeting accidentally in foreign lands... Together. The whole package. You and me." She flipped the digital pad closed and dropped the toast on the plate. She wasn't particularly hungry anyway.

"I could leave tonight. Head to Europe." Frustration edged his voice, his fingers curling into a fist.

"All right, well, when you get back, I'll be right here. Unless they change the locks..." That was definitely within his purview. "In which case, I'll be on the fourteenth floor. Did you know we have three thousand square feet? I don't think it will look remotely odd if I'm living there." She rose and leaned over to kiss him softly. "Speaking of which, I have to go to work. I love you. I hope I'll see you later."

Tucking her digital tablet under her arm, she walked to the door. She'd forgotten her purse, but she wasn't about to ruin her exit by going back for it. She let herself out and walked over to the elevator.

Kyle stood inside when it dinged open and he gave her a small encouraging smile. "You play a mean hardball, Miss Novak. Keep it up."

She grinned and they rode down silently to the fourteenth floor.

~

## ARMAND

"She's impossible." Armand paced in front of the window of the hospital room. Richard had finally been released from the surgical floor and security arranged for a private room. It would still be a few days before he could go home.

"Really? Do tell." His best friend sat up in bed, his bruised face looked like hell—the green and yellow splotches somehow uglier than the deep purple when he'd been admitted.

"She won't listen to reason. I told her I love her, I've told her I want to be with her..."

"Then listen to her." Richard interrupted the diatribe. "And point of order, I'm pretty sure the words you told me you used were 'maybe in a few months' and 'a jackass who loves you.' Of course, I'm on painkillers and you're upset. So maybe I'm wrong."

Armand glared at him. "You're extremely blasé about this. I would think after your accident..."

Opening his eyes, the attorney met his glare with a bland look. "That I'd what? Vote for you to continue to make stupid choices? I told you, you get crazy impulsive where she's concerned. You're fanatical in wanting to protect her—but has it not occurred to you that the safest place in the world is with you? All the time? You're constantly surrounded by security and as insane as I think it is, she doesn't seem to mind."

He stopped and considered that. Anna hadn't complained, not once in the entire debacle. She'd been furious with him, shot him with a Nerf gun and told him no—repeatedly. But she never complained about security.

He'd gone to New York on business, three days gone, and when he returned... "Do you know what she did last night?" He changed the subject.

"No, I'm afraid not. I was here last night, watching the 49ers get their asses handed to them by Dallas. What did she do?"

"Movie night. We've argued for four days, I leave for three and she comes in last night with wine and pizza—apparently my security takes orders from her now—and romantic comedies. We watched *The Prince and Me*, *The Princess Diaries*, and *Anna and the King*." He expected recrimination or tears or maybe even the silent treatment. But she'd welcomed him with a kiss and a reminder that movie night meant tabling everything. They snuggled together on the sofa for hours.

But he went to bed alone.

Again.

Richard laughed softly. "You are so not winning this fight with her."

"It's not funny. I want to protect her."

"Then marry her, make her a princess, surround her in personal footmen, valets and body-guards and keep her locked up in the tower. You might as well enjoy the time with her—" Richard sighed. "Seriously, you don't get it, do you?"

Frowning, Armand shook his head. "Apparently not. All I want to do is protect her and you two seem to think I'm insane."

"Maybe when she and I agree on something you should think about it too. Ten years ago it got hard—really hard for both of you—and she couldn't handle it. It's not any easier now—arguably it's harder because it's not just her privacy she might give up, it's her life—but it's hers to share with you, Armand. She's trying to show you she won't leave—not again."

He sat down, the wind going out of him. "I can't lose her, Richard. I can't."

"Then stop pushing her away. You told me that you don't let threats and the rest of the world dictate your life. You take precautions, you make informed decisions—but you don't run."

Shaking his head slowly, Armand exhaled a long, weary breath. "The threats—the ridiculousness of the press—I could handle that when it was just me. But how do I risk her?"

"You don't. She does. It's her call. You're one of the best guys I know—and one of the most stand-up. You put your life on the line, willynilly, to make sure the rest of your family was safe. You've tabled your happiness for a long time, buddy."

"You sound suspiciously like one of those romantic comedies."

"And on that note, your free consultation is up, we're starting on billable hours."

Armand laughed. "You make fun now, but sooner or later you're going to meet a woman who ties you up in knots, and we'll see who is cracking jokes then."

"Not gonna happen. I'll find me some nice secretary who thinks the boss is her meal ticket, she'll be all 'yes, sir' and 'no, sir' and 'thank you very much, sir' and we'll have four kids and a dog and a summer ranch in Wyoming." Richard snorted. "Now, get the hell out of here and find your girl, or sources close to the prince are going to report you knocked her up."

"You're an ass."

"Yes, I am." Richard leaned his head back, weariness washing over his face, and Armand rested a hand on his shoulder.

"Thank you, old friend."

"Anytime. Now go—*Sands Through Our Hourglass* is coming on and I need to know if Brittany picked Jim or Bob."

He left his friend to rest and checked with the detail still assigned to him. Richard would have to get used to their company for a while. But at least while he convalesced it wouldn't be a problem.

In the car, he drummed his fingers against his thigh and pulled out his phone. He dialed Peterson and waited. "I have a question for you."

"Yes, Your Highness?"

"How many more men would we need to make Anna's residence with my household permanent?"

"Johnson's available to head her detail. Four

men on regular rotation, four to spell them. You have enough staff to handle it for now, unless you begin traveling separately for extended periods, we wouldn't need to change much, sir."

Armand smiled. "Excellent. I need to go to the airport...and I need you and Johnson to run interference with Anna for a day or two."

"Of course, sir. Destination?"

"Kansas. But don't tell her that."

"I wouldn't dream of it, sir."

# CHAPTER 19
## ANNA

Anna put on a terrific show. She stayed focused throughout the day. The gala left them with hundreds of donations to be sorted through, thanked, and an endless array of meetings with the accountants to make sure the books matched and the donations reported. But after a week of juggling, they were ready to add another two hundred students to their initial pool of ten. The satisfaction she took in that helped ease the bitter pill of Armand's resistance. Their tug-of-war love game wore on her.

But nine days after the gala and she refused to give up. She'd told him she loved him every day. She kissed him, snuggled with him and sometimes just sat in the same room with him. It would have to be enough. Staying out of his bed turned out to be the most difficult aspect. But they'd made love before and it went south. She wanted them both on the same page, at the same time, in the same act of their relationship.

If that meant waiting, well, then she would wait.

A day of meetings outside the tower and exhaustion joined her in the elevator. Kyle rode up to the penthouse floor with her. Armand had slipped away to head out of town two days before —again. Kyle and Peterson made excuses for him, but at least this time he called. Both nights before she went to sleep, her phone rang, and they talked for an hour.

It was an improvement.

Instead of stepping off and checking the apartment, something he did when the prince was absent, Kyle remained in the elevator. She gave him a questioning look and he merely smiled. "Have a good evening, Anna."

Armand was home.

Nervous tension fluttered through her stomach, cresting a wave of anticipation and excitement. She nodded slowly. "Thank you, Kyle. You too."

The doors closed and she glanced at the apartment door. In three weeks, she went from dreading the walk into that apartment to determination to excitement and full circle back to dread. She would be okay. They would be okay. No matter what happened, if they stuck together, they would survive it and she repeated the mantra every single day and sometimes twice when she was away from the man she loved.

Closing her eyes and pressing a hand against her stomach, she pulled up a smile and strode toward the door. He was home. She could see him, touch him, kiss him and tell him she loved him.

And then they could argue... Her grin turned rueful. But she actually enjoyed exasperating him almost as much as kissing him. She opened the door and her greeting faded from her lips. Soft instrumental music played from the speakers, darkness fell outside and the lights were dim.

Over a dozen people filled the room. Her gaze fell on Armand first, where he stood exactly center. Arrayed around him were Alyx and her husband, Daniel—as well as his brothers, George and Sebastian. His mother, the Dowager Duchess Marie smiled at her. Good Lord, even his cousins, the sisters Grace, as the newspapers called them, were present, along with his aunt and uncle. Richard sat in a wheelchair at the end and on his other side were her parents, her older brothers and both younger brothers and Penny—who practically bounced with excitement.

"Good evening." Armand walked forward and took her bag to set down before catching her hands in his. "Welcome home."

"Hi." She glanced from him to all their guests and back again. Her stomach clenched and her heart thudded. A nameless, breathless fear coursed through her and she forced herself to look only at Armand...and to breathe.

"I'm a prince and a fool. The two are not mutually exclusive." Armand began. When she opened her mouth to speak, he gave her a stern look and she drew her lips together silently. He nodded approvingly. "I went to college to be a man and not a prince. I found the woman I wanted to spend the rest of my life with, but I was too young and too foolish to appreciate how sharing only a part of me with her could wound. I didn't tell her the truth. When she learned it, she lost her faith in me—not because she didn't love me—but because I lied and I forgot to treasure her. Her loss of faith and my complicity in it made me scornful and I embraced being the prince and forgot to be the man."

Tears burned in her eyes, she desperately wanted to say something, but didn't dare interrupt.

"Four weeks ago, I made some desperately foolish choices because I wanted to recapture those days—I wanted to be the man again, but I am a prince and a prince has consequences. I forced your hand to make you stay with me and then I tried to push you away. I've forgotten that even a prince can say—" and then he dropped down on one knee and gazed up at her, "—I'm sorry. I love you. I love your fire. I love your spunk. I love your determination to make a better world. I love your stubbornness and your absolute irreverence, which keeps me grounded. I am a better man with you at my side. You reminded me that I am a man and a prince. I love you, Anna Hope Novak. I don't want to live another moment of my life without you."

He released her hand and reached into his

jacket. "I have already asked your father for his blessing and he gave it—provided you say yes. I know you never asked for any of this—" He pulled out a glass slipper and her heart flip-flopped. "I know it wasn't your dream, but will you be my princess? Will you marry me and rescue me from this tower of loneliness? Will you be my wife forever and always?"

Anna clapped a hand over her mouth, the tears she tried desperately to stem trickled down her cheeks. Love swelled through her, while he stared up at her with naked want and desire in his eyes. The walls of pain and regret shattered and she swayed from the force of it.

He waited and she sniffed once. "Of course I'll marry you, you idiot."

Laughter burst through the room and Penny bounced in place, clapping.

"I will be your princess and your wife, I will stand by your side, I will smack you when you get too big for your britches and I will never walk away again. I will stand there and fight with you until we make up. It's hard to see happily ever after when you're living it—but I have been without my prince for too long. But I love you, Armand Charles Dagmar Andraste—"

He swallowed her last words in a kiss, surging up to wrap his arms around her. She clung to him, tears soaking her cheeks and laughter rippling through her. Applause filled the room around them and their family surged in to offer handshakes and hugs.

George stood before her, his disdainful expression far more sober. He inclined his head. "I hope you will forgive a younger brother's desire to protect his sibling and accept my genuine welcome to the family."

Anna gave him a quick hug and kissed his cheek. "I have two younger brothers, I know just how much of a pain they can be. Of course I forgive you."

He actually had the grace to look sheepish and returned her embrace with only a wee bit of awkwardness. Alyx replaced him and she gave her an enthusiastic hug, her husband offered a quick kiss to the cheek and then it was Penny's turn. Her sister squealed and danced around with her. Anna caught Armand's amused look as her brothers surrounded him. They shook his hand, patted him on the back, and when her eldest brother leaned close and murmured in Armand's ear, her prince nodded solemnly.

Richard winked and then Anna stood before Armand's mother. The woman gave her a long, measuring look and held out her hands. The cool kisses she delivered to each cheek offered restrained affection.

"Thank you, my dear," the Dowager Duchess Marie murmured. "Thank you for making my son happy again."

"I promise, I will try to do just that every day."

"I know you will. And you must come to Norway again and have a long visit with me. We shall become family."

"I would like that." Surprisingly, she meant it. She made her choice—Armand and his family, they were hers now. She glanced over to see Armand sitting on the arm of the chair and talking to Richard. But his gaze fastened on hers.

He mouthed one word. "Love."

She grinned and mouthed "you" back.

The lights turned up, the champagne flowed and Anna sent Penny off to talk to George about his upcoming college plans. Her mother and father began to dance. Amused, she shook her head. They never missed an opportunity.

Armand's arms slipped around her and she leaned back against his chest. "I think we can slip away now..." he murmured against her ear.

"While they are all in the penthouse?"

"Did I mention I own the whole building?"

Anna laughed and he drew her away from the gathering, the elevator waited and she hugged him as the doors closed. "I do have one question."

"Yes, my love?"

"Do I get to have the other slipper too?"

He laughed and she grinned. It wouldn't be easy, it wasn't a life she would have picked, but she couldn't imagine any other without him.

"You can have anything you want..."

And maybe happily ever after only happened in fairy tales, but she found her prince, locked away in his tower, and freed him. Together, they could slay dragons—even their own.

~

To enjoy more slow-burn tension, undercover heat, and bodyguard chemistry so intense it should come with a security detail—one-click **Some Like It Deadly**, Book 3 of *Going Royal*.

Be sure to grab these deleted scenes and slip deeper into the world of *Armand and Anna*.

# AFTERWORD

It's always a pleasure to share an old favorite with new people. If you enjoyed this, keep an eye out for more old favorites to return after I they get re-edited and updated. Also, if you want to check out more of my stuff, I can't wait to see what you think!

xoxo

Heather

Website:
heatherlong.net
Reader group:
facebook.com/groups/heatherspack

# ABOUT HEATHER LONG

I *love* books. Not just a little bit, but a lot. Books were my best friends when I was growing up. Books didn't care if I was new to a town or to a class. They were always there, my trustiest of companions. Until they turned on me and said I had to write them.

I can tell you that my own personal happily ever after included writing books. I've always said that an HEA is a work in progress. It's true in my marriage, my friendships, and in my career. I am constantly nurturing my muse as we dive into new tales, new tropes, new characters and more.

After seventeen years in Texas, we relocated to the Pacific Northwest in search of seasons, new experiences, and new geography. I can't wait to discover what life (and my muse) have in store for me.

Maybe writing was always my destiny and romance my fate. After all, my grandmother wasn't a fan of picture books and used to read me her Harlequin Romance novels.

*Follow Heather & Sign up for her newsletter:*
www.heatherlong.net
TikTok

# Also by Heather Long

**82nd Street Vandals**

Savage Vandal

Vicious Rebel

Ruthless Traitor

Dirty Devil

Shamelessly Loyal (Novella)

Brutal Fighter

Dangerous Renegade

Merciless Spy

Reckless Thief

Fierce Dancer

Dirty Dancer

**Bay Ridge Royals**

Shamelessly Loyal (Novella)

Battle Lines

Deceptive Truce

Wicked Surrender

Violent Chaos

Desperate Victory

**BLOOD Brothers**

Burn

Lure

## Blue Ivy Prep

Problem Child

Mad Boys

Party Crashers

Money Shot

## Bravo Team Wolf

When Danger Bites

Bitten Under Fire

## Cardinal Sins

Kill Song

First Chorus

High Note

Last Word

## Chance Monroe

Earth Witches Aren't Easy

Plan Witch from Out of Town

Bad Witch Rising

## Fevered Hearts

Marshal of Hel Dorado

Brave are the Lonely

Micah & Mrs. Miller

A Fistful of Dreams

Raising Kane

Wanted: Fevered or Alive

Wild and Fevered

The Quick & The Fevered

A Man Called Wyatt

**Heart of the Nebula**

Queenmaker

Deal Breaker

Throne Taker

**Lone Star Leathernecks**

Semper Fi Cowboy

As You Were, Cowboy

**Shackled Souls**

Succubus Chained

Succubus Unchained

Succubus Blessed

Shackled Souls (Omnibus)

**STANDALONES**

Kiss of Fate (w/Blake Blessing)

Taste of Karma (w/Blake Blessing)

I'll Be Home... (w/Tate James)

Overexposed (w/Tate James)

**Switchboard Duet**

Talk to Me

Don't Let Go

**Untouchable**

Rules and Roses

Changes and Chocolates

Keys and Kisses

Whispers and Wishes

Hangovers and Holidays

Brazen and Breathless

Trials and Tiaras

Graduation and Gifts

Defiance and Dedication

Songs and Sweethearts

Legacy and Lovers

Farewells and Forever

Hellos and Happily Ever Afters

**Wolves of Willow Bend**

Wolf at Law

Wolf Bite

Caged Wolf

Wolf Claim

Wolf Next Door

Rogue Wolf

Bayou Wolf

Untamed Wolf

Wolf with Benefits

River Wolf

Single Wicked Wolf

Desert Wolf

Snow Wolf

Wolf on Board

Holly Jolly Wolf

Shadow Wolf

His Moonstruck Wolf

Thunder Wolf

Ghost Wolf

Outlaw Wolves

Wolf Unleashed

www.ingramcontent.com/pod-product-compliance
Lightning Source LLC
Chambersburg PA
CBHW010934120626
46552CB00010B/3246